Raising Them, Raising Me

Breaking Generational Cycles and Finding Joy in Motherhood

Sacha Michailides

Sacha Michailides

ii

Dedication

To Kierslin & Merhye!

May you always know you were the reason I kept going,

even though I didn't know how.

Acknowledgment

I acknowledge my parents, whose foundation shaped the woman I became.

My husband, for standing beside me through the rebuilding.

And my aunt Heather and cousin Missy, who showed me by example what present, effective motherhood looks like.

Your influence lives on every page.

Table of Contents

Dedication iii

Acknowledgment iv

About the Author viii

Introduction 1

Chapter 1: The Birth of Us 2

✦ Reflection & Takeaway ✦ 8

Chapter 2: Growing Together 9

✦ Reflection & Takeaway ✦ 18

Chapter 3: Reflection 19

✦ Reflection & Takeaway ✦ 23

Chapter 4: Growing Together, Growing Apart 24

✦ Reflection & Takeaway ✦ 31

Chapter 5: Letting Go While Staying Connected 32

✦ Reflection & Takeaway ✦ 36

Chapter 6: Ordinary Adventures, Extraordinary Love 37

✦ Reflection & Takeaway ✦ 41

Chapter 7: Becoming a Safe Place 42

✦ Reflection & Takeaway ✦ 47

Chapter 8: Seasons of Growth 48

✦ Reflection & Takeaway ✦ 53

Chapter 9: Shifting Seasons 54

✦ Reflection & Takeaway ✦ 59

Chapter 10: Traditions, Sleepovers, & Growing Up 60

✦ Reflection & Takeaway ✦ 66

Chapter 11: Independence Unfolding 67

✦ Reflection & Takeaway ✦ 73

Chapter 12: Finding Myself in the Middle 74

✦ Reflection & Takeaway ✦ 79

Chapter 13: The Balance of Becoming 80

✦ Reflection & Takeaway ✦ 86

Chapter 14: Reclaiming Myself 88

✦ Reflection & Takeaway ✦ 94

Chapter 15: The Art of Letting Go & Growing 96

✦ Reflection & Takeaway ✦ 101

Chapter 16: Parenting Without Perfection 102

✦ Reflection & Takeaway ✦ 107

Chapter 17: The Grace of Imperfection 108

✦ Reflection & Takeaway ✦ 114

Chapter 18: Rediscovering Joy & Purpose 115

✦ Reflection & Takeaway ✦ 120

Chapter 19: The Woman Beneath the Roles 121

✦ Reflection & Takeaway ✦ 128

Chapter 20: Reclaiming Joy 130

✦ Reflection & Takeaway ✦ 136

Chapter 21: The Woman I Am Becoming 138

✦ Reflection & Takeaway ✦ 146

Chapter 22: Finding My Voice & Reclaiming My Joy 148

✦ Reflection & Takeaway ✦ 154

Chapter 23: When Grief Opens the Door to Deeper Healing 155

✦ Reflection & Takeaway ✦ 162

Chapter 24: When Grief Teaches You How to Live Again 164

✦ Reflection & Takeaway ✦ 170

Chapter 25: The Return to Myself........................... 171

✦ Reflection & Takeaway ✦ 177

Chapter 26: Rebuilding, Resilience, & Creative Roots 179

✦ Reflection & Takeaway ✦ 184

Chapter 27: The Quiet Becoming................................ 186

✦ Reflection & Takeaway ✦ 190

Chapter 28: Becoming the Change, We Leave Behind 191

✦ Reflection & Takeaway ✦ 196

Chapter 29: What They Will Carry Forward 198

✦ Reflection & Takeaway ✦ 203

Chapter 30: The Life I Am Choosing 204

✦ Reflection & Takeaway ✦ 207

Author's Note 209

About the Author

Sacha Michailides is a mother and writer shaped by an early life that required resilience long before she understood the word. Her upbringing included instability and unaddressed pain that quietly informed her understanding of responsibility, self-protection, and growth.

Rather than lingering in questions of fault, Sacha turned her attention inward. What mattered most was not why things happened, but what she would choose to do next. Over time, she learned that healing does not require agreement or permission. It begins with awareness and choice.

Motherhood became a defining chapter. It invited reflection, softened some truths, sharpened others, and called her into more intentional living. Through parenting, Sacha committed to breaking cycles not through blame, but through presence, boundaries, and compassion.

Raising Them, Raising Me is not a story about the past. It is a story about response. Written as a legacy for her daughters and a companion for anyone navigating generational complexity, the book explores what it means to grow without denying where you came from, and to offer grace without surrendering truth.

Sacha believes that healing is a personal responsibility, that growth is an act of courage, and that choosing differently is one of the quietest and most powerful forms of love.

Introduction

I grew up in a world where survival was a skill, not a choice: teen parents, substance struggles, abuse. I saw cycles repeat before my eyes and wondered if I was doomed to repeat them too. But here I am, years later, messy, flawed, but determined: breaking cycles, healing, and building a life that's mine.

This book isn't about perfection. It's about real life. It's about the good, the hard, the ridiculous, and what it takes to parent your children while parenting yourself. It's about the small victories, the lessons learned the hard way, and the courage it takes to choose differently from the past you inherited.

If you've ever felt trapped by your own history, overwhelmed by parenting, or unsure if healing is possible, this book is for you. It's my story, yes, but more importantly, it's a roadmap to becoming the parent and the person you were always meant to be.

Chapter 1: The Birth of Us

The night my first daughter came into the world, the room became a battlefield.

Alarms screamed. Nurses shouted codes. The sharp scent of the hospital hung in the air, mingling with the tense energy of everyone fighting for her life.

A male doctor I had never met leapt onto the delivery table, pressing into my chest, screaming, "Push!" My ribs cracked beneath him, sharp and unforgiving.

My own doctor yelled, "Stop!" and worked frantically to free the baby trapped inside me.

My husband collapsed onto my chest, trembling. His arms could not grip me through the chaos, but his lips found my neck, and he whispered into it, words of prayer, of pleading, of love. I felt the warmth of him against my skin even as my own body shook. For a moment, it grounded me amid the storm. I felt the tiny press of his hand against mine, a silent reassurance, a promise that he would not leave my side.

When she finally emerged, there was silence.

The same doctor who had seemed like a stranger revealed himself as a pediatrician and immediately began resuscitation.

Our baby had gone into cardiac arrest.

While I lay broken and bleeding, he brought her back to life.

She was rushed to the NICU. Machines breathed for her while I lay weak and poisoned by afterbirth toxemia, willing milk into breasts that refused to respond.

Her stay in the NICU was grueling. She had to remain under the light constantly, only taken out for brief, often unsuccessful attempts to breastfeed. I tried pumping, but my body refused to cooperate. I could produce only a little milk for her, and it never felt like it was enough. I watched her, tiny and fragile, and felt helplessness that settled deep into my bones. Every beep, every whir of the machines reminded me of how delicate she was and how powerless I felt. Yet even in those moments, a small smile tugged at her lips when I leaned close, a tiny grasp of my finger through the incubator glass, a reminder that she was still fighting.

Finally, when I could hold her in my arms, feeling her warmth against my chest, I whispered the name we had chosen, Kierslin. I traced her tiny fingers and counted her breaths silently, a ritual of love and protection, small gestures that felt like medicine for my heart.

Before this night, I had already cremated a child, my firstborn, whom I never got to hold in life. I had held his tiny body, feeling both the weight of him and the emptiness he left behind. In that unbearable silence, I made a promise to God. If God ever granted me children again, I would do everything in my power to be the best mother I could be.

His name was Christian.

It was a promise that demanded more than love. It demanded me, the version of me I had never dared to become. Strong enough to survive loss, resilient enough to face fear, and open enough to give love even when it might hurt.

I understood, even then, that keeping that promise would not be about perfection. It would be about transformation. Raising children would require raising myself. I had to confront my own fears, my own wounds, the cycles I had inherited, and the ways I had failed myself. Only by doing that could I hope to give my children the life I imagined for them.

And so, when she came into the world, fragile and fighting for her first breath, that promise flared inside me like a beacon. I had been broken once before, but now I have a reason to rebuild. To grow. To rise.

Becoming her mother meant becoming my own person first, strong, present, and unflinchingly real. It meant learning to mother my own heart so I could mother hers.

Four years later, another child came into the world, this time by C-section. The pain was excruciating. My body was torn open again, and my milk came in at the same time. Waves of pain hit in convulsions that reminded me of Christian's birth, making me scream and beg loudly for anesthesia. My husband hovered at my side, trying to comfort me. I did not want to hear it. I blamed him for everything, from the surgery table to the state of the universe, and he nodded along like a saint quietly absorbing my melodrama. Poor man.

And yet, unlike my first daughter, everything else seemed to fall into place. This baby was ready to go home almost immediately. She latched instinctively, feeding without struggle or concern. Watching my husband cry as he held her for the first time, I thought, this is what we missed before, the quiet miracle of simply being together, alive, and whole. I brushed a strand of her hair from his forehead, and he smiled through his tears. It was a simple, human moment that made all the fear and pain worth it.

We named her Merhye.

When Kierslin met her for the first time, she wrapped tiny arms around her and whispered that she would love her forever, to be the best big sister she could be. I held back my own tears as I watched the two of them, their small hands entwined, Kierslin giggling and Merhye smiling like they shared a joke only they understood, a tiny, perfect moment of connection and joy. In that moment, I realized we were all keeping the same promise, to become the best versions of ourselves for each other.

As the girls grew, we shared stories of Christian, our heartache, and the "what ifs." They asked questions, offered hugs, and carried pieces of that grief with us. Even now, we still speak of him, a reminder that love endures, even in absence.

Motherhood is not defined by perfection or control. It is about presence, resilience, and love. It is about showing up every day for each child, regardless of how life begins or what obstacles we face. Even amid pain, I found a rhythm, a confidence, a knowledge that I could rise to meet whatever my children needed.

This book is not about perfection.

It is about jagged edges, heartbreak, humor, tears, and the courage it takes to keep choosing love, even when life begins in pain.

✦ **Reflection & Takeaway** ✦

Trauma can mark the beginning of something sacred. The night my first daughter arrived was filled with fear, pain, and chaos, yet it revealed a strength I did not know I had. Healing often begins in moments we would never choose. Your own breaking point can also be the doorway to a deeper love and resilience.

Pause & Consider

When have you discovered unexpected strength in the middle of a crisis?

Chapter 2: Growing Together

Growing up, chaos was a constant companion. When doors slammed and voices soared with curse words, I would turn on music to fall asleep, letting melodies carry me away from the tension. If that did not work, I would pull out a pen and paper and write to God, pouring my fears, my prayers, and my longing for safety onto the page. Sometimes, I prayed silently for the person I loved most in our home, hoping somehow my words could protect her.

My siblings and I each found our roles in navigating the storm. My brother would cling to me, crying into my side whenever things escalated. My sister became the protector of our home, shielding my mother during moments of chaos and stepping in to protect me outside the house. We survived by watching each other, shielding each other, and understanding without words that love and loyalty often looked messy but mattered most of all.

Despite the turbulence, holidays were always celebrated. On Christmas Eve, we would gather in my brother's room and sing carols until he could no longer manage the noise and kicked us out. Christmas morning brought stockings made from socks, with oranges tucked into the bottoms. I always asked for dictionaries, determined to expand my vocabulary and become the spelling bee queen at school. School became my safe space, a place where my effort and focus earned me attention and recognition I often did not receive at home.

When my first son, Christian, was born, the heartbreak of losing him crystallized a promise I made to God: if I were ever given another chance, I would raise my children differently. I would nurture, protect, and love in ways I had not always received. I had to become a mother to myself first, so I could be the mother they needed.

With Kierslin, that promise began to take shape. The early NICU days were intense. I had to be transported by wheelchair due to toxemia, and the NICU felt impossibly far away. I remember looking at the other babies, so tiny and fragile, and then at my 8-pound-8-ounce baby, closer to ten pounds now thanks to IV fluids, who seemed to burst at the seams of her incubator. Every beep of the monitors reminded me of her strength and fragility at the same time. Her first grasp was not of me; it was of her father's chin. It made him laugh and cry at the same time, and in that moment, I realized parenthood was a mix of heartbreak, awe, and joy for which you could never prepare.

Every day in the NICU felt like a small victory. I learned to read the subtle shifts in her breathing, the tiny movements that signaled hunger or comfort, and the exact way to hold her without startling her. Each milestone, the first time she opened her eyes, the soft grasp of my finger, or the way she responded to my voice, felt monumental. Before being released, every baby had to complete a car seat test. When it was Kierslin's turn, the nurses joked that she did not even need it, her size alone proving she was ready. At 21 inches, she was larger than most, already a little powerhouse.

I still remember my first night in the NICU vividly. The hallway lights were dim, casting long shadows across the linoleum floor. The constant hum of machines and the rhythmic beeping of monitors created a strange lullaby. I wheeled myself from station to station, leaning over her incubator, feeling her tiny chest rise and fall. The smell of antiseptic mixed with the faint scent of baby lotion was comforting and foreign at the same time. My husband stood beside me, whispering reassurances, holding my hand, and brushing my hair back as I tried not to cry. Other parents were asleep in chairs, exhausted, some dozing with their tiny miracles in their arms. I felt a mixture of awe and fear; every breath she took was a battle won.

Four years later, Merhye arrived, and I saw how far I had come. Kierslin wanted to name her sister Shakira, and we decided to give her the chance to name her guinea pig that. We later discovered that the singer Shakira and Merhye shared a birthday. Merhye was due to be born by C-section on my husband's birthday, but we were called in for the C-section a few days early when another mom-to-be could not get there due to a terrible winter snowstorm. My husband, ever the wannabe race car driver, was determined to get me there, as I was so over being pregnant.

During Merhye's first weeks, I was told I could not carry more than five pounds. We all laughed when I told my mother she might have to move in, as Merhye had been born at 9 pounds 11 ounces and 24 inches long. My husband took off as much time as possible to stay with Kierslin and me when she was born and made to stay in the hospital, helping in every way he could. Our hospital stay was filled with moments of humor and humanity. A woman once shared a story about how loudly another woman had cried while trying to take a bowel movement after multiple stitches, and we later realized it was me. Thirty-six stitches inside and out, and that first bowel movement felt like childbirth all over again.

Merhye's first smile came the moment Kierslin grasped her tiny finger. That small, perfect connection reminded me of why I fought to be a better mother; the bonds we create as a family are often fragile, fleeting, and miraculous. Watching Kierslin embrace her sister, promising lifelong love and protection, was a quiet confirmation that the cycle could end with us. That we could choose differently.

Our bedtime ritual became a cherished tradition. Every night, I would read them a story, lingering over the pages until they fell asleep. When Merhye turned eleven, she declared she no longer wanted the stories, and though it marked the end of a ritual, it felt like a victory, a reminder of how far we had come. This was a much gentler, sweeter practice than the Dear God letters and prayers I had relied on as a child.

Parenting them has been full of small, tender, and often hilarious moments. Kierslin has a way of announcing the most random facts at exactly the wrong moment, like correcting strangers on how to pronounce Merhye while I scramble to explain it. Merhye has a mischievous streak, giggling at messes she knows she should not make, while Kierslin scolds her like a tiny teacher.

Schoolwork brings its own set of challenges. Both Kierslin and Merhye have cried when overwhelmed by studying, and I've always told them to walk away and have their moment. Nobody had paid attention to me struggling with school, but I knew they needed to feel their feelings fully before circling back. If they tried to force it while upset, they wouldn't learn anything effectively. These small lessons about patience, self-awareness, and emotional regulation are part of the gift of parenting them differently than I was parented.

Some of their humor is completely mysterious to me. They will randomly say things like, "Nothing beats a Jet 2 holiday," and my husband and I have no clue what they mean. These little one-liners remind me that their world sometimes exists in parallel to mine, full of joy and inside references I will never fully understand.

Music and movement continue to bind us. I once felt homesick, and without missing a beat, Kierslin jumped into a spontaneous booty-shaking dance break in the kitchen. Her three-year-old sister joined her, and soon we were all laughing, dancing, and falling into a moment of pure, silly joy. It was one of those simple family moments that feel infinite when you're living it.

Some mornings, Kierslin will quietly watch Merhye get ready for school, memorizing her teacher assignments to either warn her or tease her, only to forget by the time Merhye panics over homework later. There are moments when all three, my husband, Kierslin, and Merhye, will laugh at my attempts to pronounce a French word, while I scramble to keep up with their fluency. These moments of shared laughter, teasing, and playful chaos feel like the antidote to the tension of my childhood.

We often break into spontaneous musical dance moments in the kitchen. Kierslin used to lead these, especially when she sensed anyone needed a pick-me-up. Music often fills the house, and laughter follows. Unlike my childhood, when meals were often eaten separately and silently, we always try to eat together. These moments, messy, loud, and full of energy, remind me that family can feel warm, connected, and joyful.

Soccer games are another place where I show up fully. I am the parent I needed: loud, cheerful, and present on the field, cheering for every goal, consoling every miss, and celebrating the effort more than anything else. I learned that being fully present, even in the chaos, is a gift my children will carry with them long after the games are over.

Even the routines, the smell of baby lotion, the squeak of a crib, the hum of nighttime monitors, became symbols of survival, joy, and ordinary miracles. My husband's humor softens the hardest days. Even in exhaustion, his silly antics, pretending to race to get the kids ready for school, narrating bedtime stories like Donald Duck, or me over-packing snacks for every outing, turn ordinary moments into memories we will never forget. The name Dave seems to run in our family, from my father to my brother, my husband, and my sister's ex-husband, creating endless playful confusions and jokes that only we fully understand.

I have learned that healing is not linear. I still stumble. I still carry echoes of the past. But now I can recognize them, name them, and choose another path. I can parent my children while parenting myself, laughing at the ridiculous moments, crying in the messy ones, and building a life defined not by survival alone, but by love, resilience, and hope.

And in those moments, Kierslin's tiny fingers curled around her sister, Merhye's laughter echoing through our home, and my husband's playful energy at our side, I see the full circle of everything I once lost and everything I vowed to create. Our family is not perfect. It is messy, loud, beautiful, and alive. It is proof that cycles can be broken, that hearts can heal, and that love can triumph even in the shadow of past pain.

As I watched Kierslin and Merhye laugh, argue, dance, and grow, I began to see more clearly how raising them was inseparable from raising myself. Every bedtime story, every homework meltdown, every shared joke, or silly dance in the kitchen was a mirror, reflecting the parts of me I was still learning to understand and heal. Parenthood was no longer about guiding them; it was about learning who I could be when I chose patience over fear, laughter over frustration, and love over old patterns. And in that quiet, chaotic, beautiful space, I realized that the work of raising them would also be the work of raising me.

✦ Reflection & Takeaway ✦

Everyday life: kitchen dance parties, late-night homework tears, bedtime stories, all can become a form of healing. By choosing presence, patience, and humor, we rewrite the stories we were handed. You do not need a perfect childhood to create a loving family; you need the courage to show up, repeatedly, with an open heart.

Pause & Consider

What ordinary moments in your own life have quietly healed you or someone you love?

Chapter 3: Reflection

Night settles like a deep exhale. From the hallway comes the steady breathing of my daughters, a rhythm that quiets the house and slows my own pulse. In that hush, I trace the distance between the girl I once was and the woman standing here now.

Motherhood is the clearest mirror I know. It shows me how far I have come and how far there is to go. When the girls face a challenge, I am reminded that healing is practiced in ordinary moments. Instead of the silence I grew up with, I offer space for their feelings. Instead of hiding pain, we name it, even when the naming is messy.

A counselor once told me that pain can be a teacher, that there is good buried inside trauma if you are willing to dig. I doubted her until my thirty-ninth year. That was the year I stopped handing every ounce of energy to everyone else and reclaimed it for myself. I began to move my body, to nourish it, to see what strength felt like. Pounds fell away, but more important was what stayed: discipline, calm, and a quiet pride I had never known.

Change rippled outward.

The girls followed me into this new rhythm of health, sometimes at the gym beside me, sometimes cheering from the kitchen as I meal-prepped for the week. We tease and call out each other when one of us falls off track, but we always circle back. It is our silent agreement: nobody gets left behind.

I've since chased movement. Back in my corporate days, my home office doubled as a gym. Every morning, I climbed onto the elliptical for thirty minutes before work, then rolled out a mat for core workouts. Step challenges were my favorite back then; there was something satisfying about watching the numbers climb, proof that each stride mattered. That little room, now my podcast and business studio, was where I learned that consistency builds strength long before anyone sees a transformation.

These days, the workouts look different. At times, I pause my gym time to build a routine at home: weighted squats in the living room, planks in the bedroom, lunges that leave me laughing when the cat tries to "help." The girls each carve out their own space at the gym; sometimes we overlap, sometimes we don't, but we trade encouragement like it is part of the set. They're amused by how strong my legs have become and, though they may pretend otherwise, a little proud. I'm sketching out a new schedule now, ready to begin again.

My work adds its own kind of training. As a Special Education Technician, I meet storms head-on. Today, a student spun through every emotion: tears, threats, hugs, laughter, all because he wasn't first in line. Another lashed out with kicks and punches, his anger a language of its own. By the final bell, my body carried faint bruises and my heart a deeper ache. Yet those days strengthen something beyond muscle: the ability to stay grounded when chaos reaches for you.

Choosing calm has become a habit, like breathing through a difficult set at the gym. Some mornings, I still wake with old hurts pressing at the edges, but I've learned to catch myself before bitterness takes root—a slice of "humble pie," as I call it, and the weight lifts.

Later, when the house is quiet, I sit in the podcast room. The elliptical still leans against the wall, a silent witness to every version of me that has passed: from the corporate professional squeezing in thirty minutes before work, to the mother reclaiming her strength, to the woman finding her voice behind a microphone. Wires, weights, and microphones share the same floor, each a reminder that growth is never just one thing. Life is layered, and every season leaves something useful behind. The faint hum of the old machine lingers in the silence, like a heartbeat, steady and familiar proof that movement, in every form, has always been part of my story.

✦ Reflection & Takeaway ✦

Everyday choices; rolling out a mat for a quick workout, laughing with your children in the kitchen, pausing to breathe through chaos at work, becoming lessons in resilience.

Strength is not only physical; it's emotional, mental, and spiritual. By carving out time for yourself, practicing consistency, and noticing your own growth, you create a foundation that supports both you and those you love. Every small decision to show up for yourself builds a steadier, stronger life.

Pause & Consider

What small, repeated choices in your own life have helped you reclaim strength, find calm, or nurture your own growth?

Chapter 4: Growing Together, Growing Apart

Parenting is a living, breathing experiment. Every day brings chaos, joy, laughter, and lessons. Raising Kierslin and Merhye has shown me that teaching them isn't about academics or etiquette; it's about holding space for their emotions, guiding them through mistakes, and celebrating every small victory along the way.

Morning routines often felt like a circus. When the girls were younger, tea parties were a regular part of a complete breakfast with imaginary cakes, tiny cups, and elaborate rules I had to follow. One morning, I learned never to doubt Kierslin again: Merhye had shoved raisins up her nose, something Kierslin swore she had done, and I didn't believe her until Merhye sneezed them out across the kitchen table. That day, raisins were officially hazardous.

Bath time had its own challenges. The girls shared a tub, and on one memorable day, Merhye… well, she pooped. Kierslin reacted exactly how you would imagine a dramatic older sister reacting; she leapt out of the tub like a mermaid diving over the side, inadvertently kicking Merhye in the face. Laughter, disgust, and chaos all rolled into one. Even now, years later, we still joke about that "mermaid dive incident," a reminder that parenting is rarely graceful but always memorable.

The sibling bond between the girls is fierce. Anytime I correct one of them about her behavior, the other often interjects, defending her sister as though she were her personal lawyer. They tease, argue, and protect each other with loyalty that sometimes surprises me. Merhye has always been competitive, determined to match her sister's achievements, and has often surpassed them. Kierslin and Merhye push each other to excel academically, athletically, and artistically, and the friendly rivalry strengthens their drive and character. Watching them compete and celebrate together reminds me that healthy competition can be a gift when it teaches perseverance, determination, and resilience.

Academics and extracurriculars have added another layer to our family life. Both girls have excelled beyond anything I could have predicted. They were valedictorians of their elementary schools, earned countless academic and athletic awards, and have consistently demonstrated discipline and focus. Dave and I have only ever had to ground them twice: once for breaking a vase and lying about it, and once for inappropriate online behavior. Beyond that, they are remarkably well-behaved and initiative-taking, naturally driven to succeed in everything they do. Their successes didn't come from pressure; they came from consistent effort, support, and the freedom to explore both their talents and limits.

Kierslin has always been our traveler. After she graduated from high school, she visited seven countries in Europe, soaking in new cultures, languages, and experiences that shaped her into a thoughtful, independent young woman. Her participation in Med Life for humanitarian work brought her on a life-changing adventure last summer, reinforcing the values of service, compassion, and resilience. Watching her navigate the world with courage reminds me that the lessons I teach at home are taking root in ways I cannot always see.

Merhye, on the other hand, has always shone in the spotlight. She has taken on lead roles in musicals across Quebec and Toronto, captivating audiences with her talent and confidence. This past summer, she signed with a production team and wrote and recorded her own two singles in Nashville, an incredible milestone that highlights her creativity, determination, and drive. Supporting her artistic journey has required patience, flexibility, and encouragement, and seeing her achieve goals that once seemed impossible is a daily reminder that nurturing children's passions shapes not only their future but ours as parents.

I also began to see that I was doing a better job at parenting than I sometimes gave myself credit for. Their father, Dave, has always been there to drive them to events, cheer them on, and support them. Sometimes, though, there are hiccups. One day, while I was away on a school trip with Kierslin, he fell asleep and missed picking up Merhye from school. She was taken back to the office, and the principal gave me an earful but then flirted with Dave instead. That story still makes us laugh today.

Early on, Dave spanked the girls once when they misbehaved in Dollarama. I realized then that we had never discussed discipline. I pulled him aside and told him he was never to touch the girls again; we would not use violence as discipline. My parenting style is firm but loving. I do not practice "gentle parenting" in the soft sense, but I set boundaries, demand respect, and put their well-being first. Love and discipline coexist, and respect and security guide our household.

Humor remains our lifeline. Whether it's a failed attempt at a new recipe, mispronounced French words, or a spontaneous dance-off in the kitchen, laughter keeps us grounded. Inside jokes bloom from TikTok one-liners that my husband and I can't always follow. These little bursts of joy are more than entertainment; they are teaching moments in disguise, showing the girls how humor, resilience, and lightness can exist even in the middle of chaos.

Parenting is also about modeling resilience. Both girls have cried and become frustrated when schoolwork seemed impossible. Kierslin faced moments where she felt entirely overwhelmed by calculus, crying herself through the problem until she found a way to manage. Merhye, following her competitive streak, has often panicked when she didn't understand an assignment, especially if her sister had previously completed the same work. As stated before, I'll always tell them to walk away, take a breath, and return when ready. As a mother, I can give them the space to process emotions, set boundaries, and learn persistence without shame.

Our household thrives on rituals and connections. Bedtime stories, small celebrations with friends, and shared meals have become sacred moments of presence. They remind me of the power of consistency, of showing up, and of creating environments where children feel safe to explore their passions, make mistakes, and return to their families with trust intact.

Through all of this, parenting alongside Dave has shaped the girls' understanding of teamwork, problem-solving, and love. We have disagreements, but now we also show how adults can resolve conflicts respectfully. Dave has driven to countless events, cheered loudly at soccer matches, and learned the delicate art of supporting the girls without overstepping. We've become partners in demonstrating how love, structure, and humor coexist in daily life.

Raising them continues to raise me. Every temper tantrum, argument, award ceremony, and bath-time disaster teaches me patience, humility, and presence. I notice the ways I've grown through reclaiming my health, modeling resilience, and celebrating daily victories, and I see how that growth ripples outward, shaping the young women my daughters are becoming. Healing is ongoing, layered, and built not from perfection, but from consistent, loving presence.

As the girls grew older, the lessons learned inside our home began to meet the challenges of the outside world. School, friendships, extracurriculars, and real-life responsibilities demanded that they and I take everything we had practiced at home and apply it in new, often unpredictable ways. The confidence we nurtured, the boundaries we set, the humor we shared, and the resilience we built would all be evaluated in ways neither of us could have predicted.

This next chapter explores those real-world challenges: balancing work, parenting, and personal growth; navigating setbacks and frustrations; and finding ways to teach the girls resilience, responsibility, and self-worth through life beyond our living room. It's about stepping into the world fully present, guiding them while continuing to raise myself, and embracing the lessons that only life outside the safe walls of home can teach.

✦ Reflection & Takeaway ✦

Everyday life with children; tea parties, bath-time mishaps, sibling protection, healthy competition, awards, travel adventures, and kitchen dance breaks is an opportunity to practice patience, presence, and humor.

Parenting is a mirror: the way we show up for them teaches us how to show up for ourselves. By embracing imperfection, celebrating small victories, and creating rituals that matter, we build a family rooted in love, resilience, and connection.

Pause & Consider

What ordinary moments in your family or personal life have quietly taught you patience, humor, or resilience?

How can you use these moments to strengthen yourself and those you love?

Chapter 5: Letting Go While Staying Connected

The house felt different during the summer Kierslin left for Europe. Not bad, just empty in a way I hadn't expected. No last-minute rides across town, no voice drifting through the hallway asking if anyone wanted to play cards or complaining that we were "an ingredients household" with nothing ready-made to snack on. Even the air seemed quieter, like it was holding its breath.

Preparing her for that trip felt like a ceremony of small goodbyes. We opened a credit card, gathered different currencies, and set up an international SIM so she could check in. I watched her tuck her passport into a little zippered pouch and knew, even as I fussed over the details, that it might be the last time she'd need me so completely. When I hugged her goodbye at the airport, nerves and excitement tangled together.

Every call became a postcard I could hear. She'd start with her signature "OMG, Mom, guess what happened today!" and then unfurl stories of the red-light district, friends getting drunk in Amsterdam, climbing the Austrian Alps, visiting Anne Frank's house and a concentration camp, watching World Cup matches in crowded squares, and rooting for France because it was her father's birthplace. Each story stretched the space between us and, strangely, pulled us closer.

Not long after, Merhye headed to New York City for her own adventure. She navigated subway lines and landmarks with a confidence that startled me: Grand Central Station, the Intrepid Museum, the Natural History Museum, even a night in Hell's Kitchen before taking in a musical about Alicia Keys, fitting since she's shaping her own music career now. Around the same time, Kierslin was in Ecuador with Med Life on a humanitarian trip that left her more grounded and humbler. My phone lit up with photos and quick messages: a mountain sunrise from one, a Broadway marquee from the other. I felt proud and a little breathless watching them step into their wide worlds.

Their independence reminded me of my own. Years earlier, a corporate job had sent me to seven different states, the first time I'd ever traveled alone. I'd meet colleagues after work, especially one who became a kind of soulmate in business, a partner who challenged my thinking and kept my ambition sharp. Days were full of lively conversations and extensive ideas; nights were the hardest. Hotel rooms were too quiet, the sounds unfamiliar. Dave and I would talk on the phone like teenagers until one of us drifted off. If he fell asleep first, I'd let the TV play softly or put on music until the strangeness of the room faded. I learned then that I could be self-sufficient and still deeply connected.

When the girls grew more independent, Dave and I began rediscovering each other. Our first mini getaway was to a cabin on the lake we'd visited long ago. We left the girls home alone for the first time, stocked the fridge, and drove off with equal parts freedom and nerves. For two days, we stayed in our pajamas, cooking, watching movies, making love, and playing games, simply reconnecting. It wasn't extravagant, but it felt like oxygen for our marriage.

More than three decades together, dating since I was fifteen and he was seventeen, have given us layers of history. We've survived a youth shelter, living in a shady motel room, and nights on borrowed couches. We've pushed each other through college and out of old wounds. I've always been the one more driven to heal; he sometimes gets stuck in ruts, maybe because he's estranged from his family back in France. Yet even with our starts and stops, we keep choosing each other, finding ways to grow side by side.

As the girls spread their wings, my pride mixes with fear. I still picture them as toddlers when I read the news about late-night subway incidents or see headlines about women disappearing. I want them to taste freedom without danger, to roam the world without carrying my worries. I don't say this aloud often, but it's there, the quiet hope that the world will be kind.

And yet every time I watch them win, whether it's Merhye's music career taking off or Kierslin hiking an alpine trail halfway across the world, I see proof that the work of raising strong, independent women is worth every nervous prayer. I wanted them to be bold and self-reliant, and they are. The echoing house, the long-distance calls, the quiet evenings with Dave, these are the gentle reminders that letting go is not losing; it's loving in a wider circle.

✦ **Reflection & Takeaway** ✦

Letting go is a daily practice, not a single event. We prepare our children for independence, but we also prepare ourselves to keep loving them from a distance. Pride and fear can coexist, and intimacy can grow even in the spaces apart.

Pause & Consider

Where in your own life are you invited to release control over a child, a partner, or even a younger version of yourself, so that growth can happen on both sides?

Chapter 6: Ordinary Adventures, Extraordinary Love

Life with Dave has always been a blend of grit and laughter, a living reminder that love isn't built on sweeping gestures but on the quiet, daily choice to stay. After decades together, we've learned that the moments we remember most are rarely the ones we planned. They're the ones that sneak up on us, turning inconvenience into memories and ordinary afternoons into something we still talk about years later.

Take our latest adventure. Dave, convinced that YouTube videos could turn him into a certified mechanic, decided to manage our oil changes himself. When that went well, he grew bolder and tackled the brakes on his own car. He emerged from the driveway with grease on his hands and a grin of pure triumph. A week later, we set off on a couple's road trip to visit a cluster of small Ontario towns, one of which had been named "the cutest town in Ontario" by some travel blogger. We were barely an hour in the drive when a metallic clatter shot through the car. A chunk of brake flew off and skittered across the pavement like a warning from the universe.

My heart leapt into my throat. I was ready to panic, but Dave stayed calm, easing the car onto the shoulder with the patience of a saint. Normally, he drives like a maniac, his heavy foot on the gas, the spark of countless arguments and even a few brief break-ups back in the day. This time, he was serene, joking as we limped to the nearest dealership. The mechanic took one look and told us the repair was covered free of charge. Dave just smiled, unbothered. Meanwhile, I sat in the waiting room, getting hungrier and crankier by the minute, hormones running wild. The roles had flipped: the man who usually fuels my anxiety was the calm anchor, and I was the storm.

The rest of that getaway followed the same rhythm: quiet surprises stitched with small joys. We wandered Cobblestone streets, ducked into antique shops, and shared warm pastries at a café where the barista insisted we try the town's famous pizza. We played cards in the hotel room and laughed at how competitive we still are after all these years. It wasn't a grand vacation, but it felt like exactly what we needed: a reminder that our marriage thrives not on luxury but on togetherness.

Back home, our life carries that same mix of chaos and comfort. This past summer, I launched a solo podcast about healing. I call it my "hot mess" project because it's unpolished and full of rambling tangents, but it's mine. I hit record, pour my thoughts into the microphone, and figure things out as I go. Dave cheers me on from the sidelines, even if he doesn't quite understand why strangers might want to listen to me talk through my feelings. Sometimes, he'll peek into my little podcast room, the same space that once doubled as a home gym and office, and offer to make coffee before I start an episode.

At night, we return to our quiet rituals. Dave will stretch out beside me and trace slow, lazy circles on my back until I drift to sleep. Some nights, he keeps it up for minutes; other nights for hours, a silent conversation that needs no words. But when his snoring begins, it's a deep, thunderous rumble, and I inevitably grab the remote to raise the head of the bed until he hunches forward and the sound cuts off. There are nights I secretly wish he'd stay in the living room forever just so I can sleep, but the truth is I miss him when he isn't there. The warmth of his arm draped across me, the comfort of his steady breath, it's worth the midnight interruptions.

These small patterns are what hold our decades together: brake dust on the roadside, shared pastries in a sleepy town, the buzz of a podcast mic, the quiet dance of back tickles and snoring negotiations. They prove that love doesn't depend on flawless plans or constant romance. It's built in everyday life: the repairs that fail, the trips that detour, the bedtime rituals that never quite go as intended. It's choosing each other repeatedly, even when the brakes fall off, literally and figuratively.

✦ **Reflection & Takeaway** ✦

Long love isn't about perfection; it's about the courage to stay curious and keep showing up. It's the patience to laugh when plans unravel, the humility to apologize when tempers flare, and the joy of finding adventure in the ordinary.

Pause & Consider

What small rituals, shared meals, inside jokes, even little irritations quietly keep your closest relationships alive?

When life throws a detour, can you pause long enough to see the story you'll one day laugh about?

Chapter 7: Becoming a Safe Place

Bedtime, when I was little, wasn't soft or soothing. It wasn't a time to unwind or whisper goodnight. It was the hour when walls felt too thin, when voices carried too easily, and when fear had nowhere else to go but into the quiet spaces of a child's mind.

My brother would sometimes scream about the man in the closet. His voice still echoes in my memory, panicked, trembling, desperate for someone to believe him. It was the flicker of a light turning on at night or the faint sound of movement that made his imagination spin. Or, like all of us, he just needed a place to put his fear.

My sister and I would chatter through the noise about school, about music, about nothing at all, anything to fill the air with something other than the sounds we didn't want to hear. Sometimes, we'd play our favourite songs until we drifted off, the music wrapping around us like a fragile kind of protection. The melodies became our lullabies, the lyrics our shield.

When I think back now, I realize we were trying to build a sense of safety with what little we had. Two little girls whispering in the dark, learning early how to comfort themselves when the world felt unpredictable.

As we got older, that need for comfort found its way into other things. My sister and I would fight over the phone, who got to talk to their boyfriend, who needed the connection more that night. On the evenings she didn't have anyone, I'd stay up on the phone until morning, the sound of someone's voice on the other end keeping me company until I fell asleep. I didn't realize it then, but what I was searching for wasn't love; it was calm—a steady, predictable sound. Someone staying, even if it was only through a wire.

I learned earlier that connection could be a kind of safety, that the sound of another person breathing beside you, even through static, could make the dark feel less heavy.

When I became a mother, I promised myself that bedtime would mean something different for my children. I wanted to rewrite that part of the story. I wanted their nights to end in peace, not tension; with warmth, not worry. So, I began the ritual of reading them a story every night.

It wasn't about books, really. It was about presence, about sitting on the edge of their beds, watching their eyes grow heavy, knowing that their last thought before sleep would be a soft one. Some nights they'd pick the same story again, and

I'd read it like it was brand new, because I understood that sometimes we just need to hear the familiar.

For years, I read to them until they drifted off, the rhythm of my voice becoming their safety, and in a way, mine too. Those moments healed a part of me I didn't even know was still open. That's what motherhood does: it gives you a second chance to give what you needed, and to receive it, quietly, in return.

Then one night, sometime in Merhye's eleventh year, she asked me not to tuck her in anymore. I stood in the doorway, holding the moment in my chest like a fragile keepsake. There was pride and grief, too. The kind that only comes when you realize that your children are growing not away from you, but beyond you. She didn't need my presence to feel safe anymore, and that was the most beautiful heartbreak.

Over the years, our family built new rituals, ones wrapped in laughter, togetherness, and tradition. Every Christmas Eve, the girls would open a special gift that we always told them was from Dodo, Dave's brother. Inside was a movie, treats, and matching Christmas pajamas. They'd rip the paper with the same excitement every year, even though they already knew what was inside. We'd curl up together, watch

The Polar Express, and stay up far too late, surrounded by the glow of the tree and the quiet hum of belonging.

It became our thing. Our proof that love doesn't have to be loud or complicated; it can live in the simple act of being together.

A couple of years ago, we began to outgrow even that tradition. The girls were older, and we wanted something different, something that reflected who we were becoming. In 2023, we decided to celebrate Christmas in New York, Home Alone style. We wandered through the city streets, marveling at the lights, laughing over hot chocolate, and soaking in every moment. It felt like a movie, chaotic, magical, and deeply ours.

Last year, we spent Christmas in Pittsburgh, bundled in scarves and black-and-yellow, watching the Steelers play the Chiefs on Christmas Day. It wasn't traditional, but that was the point. We were drafting a new story together. This year, we'll be away again; another adventure waiting to unfold, another chapter in the quiet promise I made to build something different for my family.

Sometimes this is what healing really looks like: not in big, dramatic breakthroughs, but in the quiet rewriting of what once hurt. It's in the rituals, the laughter, the softness you choose when you could have repeated the chaos you came from.

Healing isn't about pretending the past didn't happen. It's about deciding that it won't happen again. It's choosing gentleness where there was once shouting. It's tucking your children into peace, even when you weren't given that yourself.

It's realizing, one ordinary night at a time, that the safe place you always needed has become the home you've created and the person you've become.

✦ Reflection & Takeaway ✦

Becoming a safe place for someone else often begins with becoming a safe place for yourself. Healing isn't about erasing the past or pretending fear didn't exist; it's about creating rituals, presence, and love that rewrite what safety feels like.

Pause & Consider

What small, repeated actions in your own life create safety and comfort for yourself or those you love?

Which rituals, bedtime stories, shared laughter, or simple acts of care can transform ordinary moments into spaces of healing, trust, and belonging?

Chapter 8: Seasons of Growth

Life in our home has always moved to the rhythm of effort, achievement, and connection. It's a rhythm that begins mid-morning, carries through lunch and dinner, and continues into the quiet moments of reflection at the end of the day. These rhythms are stitched together by shared meals, laughter, performances, and games, a foundation that celebrates presence, persistence, and support.

Dance has always been at the heart of Kierslin and Merhye's lives. They started dancing at two years old, exploring movement, music, and expression. By five, they transitioned into hip hop, a style that allowed them to develop discipline, rhythm, and individuality. Dance became both an outlet and a shared passion, one that taught them resilience, creativity, and confidence. Kierslin, now eighteen, continues to dance with expertise and elegance, while Merhye, 14, follows closely behind, blending skill with ambition and a drive for the spotlight. Over the years, their dedication has taken them from creative toddler classes to elaborate routines, performances, and the stage of the theatre. Dance is not just a hobby; it's a language through which they communicate, challenge themselves, and express joy.

Sports have added another layer of growth and resilience. Kierslin had always played competitive soccer, and Merhye followed suit. On the first day of her grade 11 season, during pre-game practice, Kierslin kicked the ball and, BOOM, tore her ACL. She was on the field with her team, and the instant changed everything. Yet she managed it with remarkable calm, navigating the long nine-month recovery with emotional steadiness. Dave and I let her guide her rehabilitation, trusting that only she could understand her body's limits and emotional readiness. She approached each milestone with quiet determination, choosing when to push herself and when to rest, understanding that recovery was her own journey.

Meanwhile, Merhye continued to excel in both soccer and rugby. She not only played, but she thrived, earning MVP awards in both sports and taking on the responsibility of team captain in soccer. Every game was a testament to her talent, work ethic, and leadership. Even when Kierslin could not play, she offered advice, pointers, and encouragement, demonstrating the strength of their bond and the power of mentorship between sisters. The girls' athletic achievements were mirrored in their dedication to each other, their mutual support evident in every practice, game, and celebration.

Stage performances and musicals also marked their growing years. Kierslin performed on stage once in Mary Poppins for school, stealing the show. Beyond that, her stage presence has been focused on dance performances. Merhye, inspired by her sister, performed in Stagecoach productions and school musicals, including Mary Poppins and The Ginger Girl. She absorbed lessons from Kierslin's performances, borrowing and improving on ideas to create her own standout moments. Merhye consistently earned lead roles, collected multiple awards, and eventually signed with a production team in the U.S., culminating in her first singles recording in Nashville this past summer. Over her last two high school years, she amassed seven awards, following five the previous year, marking her as a top achiever academically and artistically.

Amid the whirlwind of sports, dance, and performances, family rituals anchored our days. We never ate breakfast together, but dinner became a sacred space. I chose healthy meals rich in protein to fuel their active lives. Occasionally, Dave or Kierslin would complain about the repetition of meals. Kierslin once decided to cook for herself, only to prepare the same meal every day. These meals were more than nutrition; they were moments of presence, laughter, and connection amidst busy schedules. They offered a consistent pause, a daily reminder that our family's bond is nourished in both small and substantial ways.

The girls' relationship has been a blend of competition, encouragement, and care. They cheer for each other, share strategies, and celebrate victories, both big and small. When Kierslin was recovering from her ACL, she still offered pointers for Merhye's soccer practices. Even with missed performances, Merhye, when she took a term off thinking she was done with dance, and Kierslin, while away on a humanitarian trip in Ecuador, and when she was recovering from ACL surgery, they never stopped supporting each other. These moments of encouragement, advice, and quiet presence have strengthened their bond and shaped the values they carry into every new challenge.

Every game, rehearsal, and performance has been an opportunity to witness their growth. Dave and I attend as many games and performances as possible, watching the energy, determination, and skill that define them. Each trophy, award, and lead role is not just a symbol of achievement but also a testament to years of dedication, mentorship, and perseverance. The echo of cheering fans, the rhythm of music, and the focused silence of competition fill our home with a sense of purpose and celebration.

Through dance, sports, stage, and daily routines, Kierslin and Merhye have cultivated resilience, ambition, and care. They have learned that growth is not measured only by accolades or awards, but by effort, empathy, and the courage to keep showing up for themselves and for each other. Our family rituals of shared meals, quiet conversations, celebrations, and encouragement all serve as the invisible framework supporting their journeys. They remind me that love is most powerful when it is present, consistent, and nurturing, even amid the chaos of busy lives.

At the heart of it all is the understanding that every milestone, every award, every shared lunch, or dance rehearsal contributes to the mosaic of who they are becoming. Kierslin and Merhye are thriving because they are guided by love, supported by presence, and inspired by each other. In this home, amid routines, achievements, and challenges, the greatest success is watching them grow into confident, resilient, and compassionate young women.

✦ Reflection & Takeaway ✦

Growth is built not only on victories but on consistent effort, guidance, and presence. Resilience is the quiet courage to face challenges, recover, and continue supporting one another.

Pause & Consider

How do your daily routines create stability, growth, and resilience in your family or community?

In what ways can encouragement, advice, and shared effort strengthen bonds and cultivate achievement?

Which small, consistent acts like shared meals, coaching, cheering, or practicing together leave a lasting impact on those you love?

Chapter 9: Shifting Seasons

There's a certain kind of quiet that settles into a home after years of chaos, not an empty silence, but a softer rhythm. It's the kind of quiet you don't notice right away. It creeps in slowly, replacing the constant hum of "what's next?" with moments where you can hear yourself think.

When the girls were little, it felt like there was no such thing as stillness. Every corner of the house carried their voices: their laughter, their footsteps, their little stories filling the air. Every plan Dave and I made revolved around nap times, dance rehearsals, or soccer games. Back then, our house was always full. It was the heartbeat of our lives.

These days, the rhythm is changing. The girls have their own lives, their own plans, their own stories that sometimes unfold far away from home. And while we still eat dinner together whenever we can, the evenings don't always belong to us as a family anymore. There are jobs, friends, dances, and games. Sometimes I look around the table and notice who isn't there. It's not sadness; it's just the shape of a new season.

When they were little, weekends meant activities and traditions. We had the kind of house where music played often, and the living room could turn into a stage at any moment. We even built them an actual stage in the basement, a little corner of the house where magic happened daily. The girls would pull out costumes from their dress-up chest, grab the microphones with their name sleeves on them, and demand that we sit down for their performance.

Their friends were never safe from it either. Even the shy ones were quickly swept into the current, performing songs and skits, giggling so hard they could barely sing. I can still hear them saying, "Mom, turn on the music!" and then watching as the basement turned into their very own concert hall. Those nights were loud and warm, a kind of everyday magic that only happens in childhood.

And then there were the group sleepovers. Every holiday, every excuse for a celebration, our house would fill with kids. Pillows, blankets, pizza, music, and endless laughter. They'd pile into their room, whispering and giggling well into the night, and I loved every second of it. Even when things broke, like the time they shattered a vase and thought hiding it would save them from being grounded. It wasn't the vase that mattered. It was the lie. When I found out, I reminded them gently that honesty would have been enough.

Even then, we were learning how to navigate growing together.

Life wasn't always noisy, though. There were quiet moments of tenderness between them. When one was sick, the other instinctively became a little nurse, offering cuddles, whispering comfort, always showing up for each other. That bond has threaded through every stage of their lives.

Before kids, Dave and I were the couple who lived in nightclubs on the weekends. Loud music, sweaty dance floors, and late nights were normal. We were young, wild, and free, and we loved it. Then parenthood came, and for years, "us" became wrapped around "them." Not out of loss, but out of love. Our identities changed, just like they were supposed to.

And now, we've arrived at a season where we've rediscovered ourselves again.

With the girls older, we can slip away together in a way we couldn't before. Date nights have become their own little rituals. Dave's idea of fun is a night at the casino, while mine is a weekend getaway. We've learned to meet in the middle, sometimes with road trips, sometimes with nights away at a cabin where it's just the two of us, no schedules, no noise, no responsibilities waiting at the door.

This past April, we took our first week-long trip away without the girls to the Dominican Republic. My mom (Grammy to the girls) came to stay with them since it was Easter. I made sure the turkey was ready, the fixings were laid out, and there were Easter treats tucked away for them. They were fine without us. That realization landed softly in my chest: they were growing, and so were we.

The trip was unforgettable. We celebrated 31 years together under the sun, something we couldn't have done years ago when their little hands still needed ours. We went to Coco Bongo, danced like teenagers again, and spent an evening at Chic Cabaret, where everything shimmered with a kind of magic only vacation can hold.

Our butler surprised us with a bottle of champagne, rose petals scattered across the bed, a filled tub, and a box of chocolates. It felt like a romantic movie, just us, no interruptions. Dave got sunburned the first day and paid for it the next when we went snorkeling. Five minutes in, hungover from the night before and wincing at the burn, he bailed out of the water. I floated above the coral with my life jacket on, laughing. It was perfectly us, a little chaotic, a lot of love.

One of our favorite places has always been Lac a la Truite. It's a tiny apartment with a fireplace and a hot tub; the kind of place that makes you fall in love with quiet. We first went for my birthday in October one year, then Dave's in February one year. Crisp air, soft snow, fire cracking, and no sound but our laughter. Those weekends remind us of who we are together outside of being parents.

The weekend after we returned from the Dominican, the girls were off again, scattered between their own adventures, friends, and lives. When they finally came home, the house filled up like someone had turned the volume back on. The front door opened, shoes hit the floor, laughter spilled down the hallway, and stories tumbled over each other like they always have.

I stood in the kitchen, listening, and felt it: this was what we'd built. A home that breathes in seasons. Loud and wild. Soft and quiet. A love that bends and grows but never breaks.

Dave caught my eye and didn't have to say a word. We both knew it. We had built something steady. Something strong enough to hold it all, the early years of noise, the quiet of rediscovery, and the beauty of watching our girls step into their own lives.

This isn't the end of a story. It's just another beginning.

✦ **Reflection & Takeaway** ✦

The seasons of life don't announce themselves; they simply arrive. One day, the house is full of tiny feet, the next it's quiet enough to hear your own heartbeat. And in that space, something new begins, not emptiness, but expansion.

Pause & Consider

What parts of yourself have you rediscovered as life shifted?

How do your relationships grow when the noise fades, and space opens?

What traditions from your past have built the foundation for the love that holds everything together now?

Chapter 10: Traditions, Sleepovers, & Growing Up

By the time the girls were in second grade, homework routines had become much smoother. I insisted they stay on top of their academics, and our summer bridging programs kept them challenged and disciplined, ensuring they remained at the top of their classes. Merhye and Kierslin also took keyboarding lessons, Merhye when she was five, Kierslin when she was nine, which added another layer of structure to their growing routines.

Our holiday traditions became an anchor for the family. Each year, the weekend before Halloween, we carved pumpkins. Some years, we experimented with painting pumpkins or adding glow-in-the-dark stickers. Carving pumpkins with intricate picture cut-outs often proved a challenge, and the girls sometimes bit off more than they could chew. They would select designs online that took over an hour to complete, while the rest of us finished ours in 20 minutes. Easter was celebrated with egg dyeing and Easter egg hunts, carefully designed to make the experience magical, even when rain forced us indoors. One year, we filled the bathtub with colorful Easter grass and glow sticks, and the girls delighted in hunting for eggs in the dark, each with her designated color.

The Elf on the Shelf became a December tradition, beginning the first weekend of the month alongside putting up the Christmas tree. Dave would lift the girls to place the star on top while I captured the moment in pictures. Even the Tooth Fairy was always a steadfast belief, adding to the enchantment of childhood.

Sleepovers were a major part of our family life. The living room or bedrooms would fill with sleeping bags and laughter as friends spilled in from every corner of the house. Sleepovers often included themed board games, movies, and specially prepared food, bunny-shaped cakes, mummy-wrapped hot dogs, graduation cupcakes, and other playful treats for each holiday or birthday theme. Sometimes, the girls would stay up all night, while other times the excitement of having friends over created nooks of sleeping bags tucked into every corner, even spilling into our bedroom. One evening, Merhye crawled into bed with us, exhausted but giggling at the chaos around her.

The sleepovers were not just fun; they were moments of teaching and growth. Merhye's younger years' best friend, Charley, who is diabetic, required careful monitoring of her insulin, and Merhye instinctively adjusted her eating patterns to match Charley's schedule, showing a remarkable empathy for others even as a young child. These experiences nurtured independence, responsibility, and compassion in both girls, lessons that would resonate well into their teen years.

Birthday parties became an extension of the girls' creativity and personalities. Kierslin once had a spa sleepover, inviting a new girl who had never attended a sleepover or birthday party before. All Kierslin's friends welcomed her warmly and promised to include her in their own celebrations. Another year, Kierslin requested that lunch bags be decorated for the homeless, and all her friends enthusiastically agreed, turning a party into an act of kindness. Merhye's kindergarten Princess Sofia party, however, taught me about her independent streak: after just 45 minutes, she went to her room, insisting everyone else leave. I had to calmly explain that the party was a two-hour event, and that we would "struggle it out together." Even these small challenges were opportunities to teach patience, negotiation, and self-expression.

The girls' independence extended to daily routines as well. They made their beds every morning without reminders until high school, when Merhye's habits began to mirror patterns her father and I once had as teenagers. Yet, despite these small rebellions, they consistently demonstrated remarkable self-discipline in academics, creative projects, and friendships.

Sleepovers, holiday preparations, and birthday parties were rarely about fun; they also involved planning and organization. I found myself preparing themed foods, organizing craft activities like pillowcase painting or scrapbooking, and overseeing chef-themed parties where the girls and their friends would create their own meals. The house would buzz with energy, laughter, and the occasional chaos that comes when a dozen children are packed into a space built for far fewer.

Their creativity and imagination thrived through music and performance. They would perform plays on the stage we built in the basement, often inviting friends along. Board games were a constant favorite, offering both competition and camaraderie. Even shy friends quickly came out of their shells, inspired by the energy of our home. The girls' natural leadership and social skills flourished in these settings, strengthened by the routines, rules, and love we consistently provided.

Vacations and trips also became an integral part of family life. March breaks were reserved for adventures, some planned and some filled with playful surprises. One year, we tricked the girls into believing we were going to Miami, only to reveal on the way that Disney World awaited them. We handed each girl a Minnie Mouse cup during a lunch stop at McDonald's to make the revelation even more magical. These trips reinforced a sense of family togetherness, exploration, and joyful surprise. Kierslin's best friend, Annabelle, became like a third daughter, traveling with us on these trips and sharing in the traditions, adding another layer of connection to our family life.

Even amid all the fun, the years were not without challenges. Parenting required flexibility and patience, particularly when it came to understanding the girls' moods, friendships, and independent desires. The balance between structure and freedom was delicate: homework, bridging programs, and routines had to coexist with sleepovers, vacations, and creative projects. Yet, through it all, laughter, kindness, and the girls' sense of wonder remained central.

The traditions we built, sleepovers, holiday rituals, birthday celebrations, and creative projects, provided a foundation for the girls to grow with confidence, compassion, and imagination. These years were defined by the joy of childhood, the lessons learned in togetherness, and the simple magic of family life in motion. Every pumpkin carved, every birthday celebration, every sleepover, and every holiday tradition became a building block in the rich tapestry of our family, moments that will forever shape who they are and how we move forward together.

✦ Reflection & Takeaway ✦

Childhood is a mosaic of routines, celebrations, and small acts of creativity. What seems ordinary at the time, carving pumpkins, sleepovers spilling across every corner, decorating lunch bags for the homeless, shapes the way children learn about empathy, independence, and the joy of shared experiences.

Pause & Consider

How do your family traditions create a sense of stability and belonging?

In what ways do everyday rituals teach resilience, compassion, and creativity?

How can moments of organized chaos, such as sleepovers, birthday parties, and holiday preparations, be seen as opportunities for growth, connection, and love?

Chapter 11: Independence Unfolding

Independence didn't arrive in a single moment; it came slowly, quietly, and unnoticeably at first. It snuck in during mornings when beds were left unmade, and alarms were ignored. It came in the way they carried themselves, the way their laughter deepened with new experiences, and the way the house itself began to feel a little different as their world grew bigger than the walls that raised them.

It began when they entered high school in grade 7. The rhythm of childhood started to shift, softening around the edges. Kierslin, who had always been neat and organized, started sleeping in later and leaving her bed a tangled mess of blankets. It wasn't laziness; it was a quiet signal of growing independence, a new sense of ownership over her time and space. Merhye, on the other hand, had never been particularly tidy. She was always too busy chasing dreams and diving into activities. Cleaning only happened when I asked. But what she lacked in tidiness, she made up for with drive. Both girls were carving out their own ways of moving through the world.

A major turning point came when they started working. At just fourteen, they both got jobs at the local grocery store, a decision that gave them more than just paychecks. It gave them independence. They learned the value of hard work, responsibility, and making choices with their own money. They began paying for anything that wasn't essential, little luxuries, outings with friends, the things that helped shape their personal style and identity. The pride they felt when buying something for themselves was written all over their faces. These weren't just transactions; they were steps toward adulthood.

For Kierslin, another major moment came at the end of high school. She traveled to Europe for two weeks, exploring seven countries with her peers. It was her first time so far from home, free to make her own choices, surrounded by friends, music, and endless unfamiliar places. She came home changed, not drastically, but with a new light in her eyes, a new layer of independence woven into who she was becoming. That trip taught her not just about the world, but about herself.

Today, both girls balance friendships, work, and school with a grace that humbles me. Kierslin has a boyfriend now, and like any young love, it takes time and energy. Merhye pours herself into her passions with unwavering determination. She plays soccer both at school and in a competitive league for our local club. She shines in theatre, collaborates closely with a vocal coach to chase her dream of becoming a recording artist, and plays rugby for her school. And both girls continue with hip hop, the same rhythm that's been part of their lives since they were little. Their schedules are full, but they've learned how to juggle it all without losing sight of what matters most.

And what matters most, to my heart, is how they still choose family. As I write this the night before my birthday, both girls are planning to be available to be with me, not out of obligation, but because they want to. That, more than anything, tells me we did something right.

Letting go was not always easy. One of the hardest adjustments for me was letting them sleep over at friends' houses. I always trusted them, but I didn't trust the unknowns of other homes. I never knew what might happen when they were out of my sight. For years, I held on tightly, keeping their sleepovers at home where they felt safe. Merhye didn't mind; she preferred being home. As she got older, she didn't really have one best friend anymore, but rather several groups of friends, including her theatre crew, who kept in close touch.

Eventually, I had to give them that freedom. I had to let them go, even if my heart clenched every time they walked out the door with an overnight bag. And while it was hard, it also marked a beautiful shift. Their sleepovers at home evolved, too. Gone were the chaotic nights of stuffed animals and matching pajamas. Instead, there were themed gatherings and murder mystery parties, yet still fun, but with a new kind of maturity. They may have grown up, but they never truly outgrew the joy of coming together.

Dave and I adjusted, too. As they grew more independent, we suddenly found ourselves with more free time. Our evenings no longer revolved around bedtime routines. Instead, we have space to breathe, to rediscover ourselves as a couple. There were moments of quiet pride and others of quiet ache. I felt it when they stopped doing certain things, like when they both quit keyboarding lessons. It was bittersweet, like watching a door close softly behind them.

Some moments of growing up came with more impact. Kierslin tearing her ACL and giving up soccer was one of them. She loved the game, but deep down, she was already ready to let it go. Still, it was a substantial change, one that reminded me just how quickly life shifts when they grow older.

Then there were the conversations. The once-simple talks about crayons and recess turned into talks about bodies, periods, and hormones. I still remember little Kierslin asking Dave why he never let her in the bathroom when he peed. She was simply curious, learning what made boys and girls different. That innocence eventually gave way to one of the hardest conversations of all, talking about sex. Dave wasn't ready. He struggled because it wasn't just a conversation about biology. It was about his little girl stepping into a world he remembered all too well as a young man. But we had that conversation with honesty and respect, and she met it with the same.

Discipline was never a big issue in our home. We made sure to raise our girls with self-discipline, and it worked. They learned early on how to manage their time, their responsibilities, and their goals. But more importantly, we taught them to be kind and humble. As a family, we did missions of service, feeding the homeless, helping those in need, and offering our hands where we could. These weren't just volunteer opportunities. They were lessons in empathy, compassion, and gratitude.

Now, as young women, those lessons live in them. They're kind. They're grounded. They're resilient. And they're strong in ways that make my heart swell.

Watching them grow up hasn't been about losing my little girls. It's been about witnessing them become exactly who they were meant to be. There are still nights when I miss the sound of them running through the house, the way sleepovers used to fill every room with shrieks and laughter. But I also love the quiet strength of who they are now. Independence hasn't pulled them away from us; it's only made our bond deeper.

They still come home. They still choose family. And I wouldn't trade that for anything.

✦ Reflection & Takeaway ✦

The shift from childhood to adolescence isn't a single event; it's a series of quiet transitions. The unmade beds, late mornings, first paychecks, and newfound freedoms all weave together into something bigger: a growing sense of self.

Independence doesn't erase connection. When the foundation is strong, it simply creates new ways to love, trust, and grow together.

Pause & Consider

How has your role changed as your children step into their independence?

In what ways can giving them space also deepen your connection?

How can trust and shared history become the foundation for this new season of growth?

Chapter 12: Finding Myself in the Middle

Parenting teenagers and young adults is like navigating a river that constantly shifts its course. Merhye, at fourteen, is chasing her dreams of fame, balancing theatre, vocal coaching, competitive sports like soccer and rugby, and hip hop, while Kierslin, at eighteen, manages work, friends, and her scientific ambitions. Their independence grows daily, and with it, I find myself walking a delicate line between support and stepping back, all while trying to figure out who I am beyond being their mother.

Watching Merhye pursue her passion for music is exhilarating and terrifying at the same time. I've had to remind myself not to live vicariously through her, to resist the temptation to relive my own unfulfilled dreams of fame. I remember auditioning for Canadian Idol and La Voix, and then seeing the same judge, Farley Flex, now evaluating Merhye at CMTC, which was surreal. Her meeting with the production companies that gave her a callback was thrilling but also a stark reminder that my ambitions must remain mine, not hers. The lesson is difficult but profound: my greatest success is not fame or accolades, it is my girls.

This realization has not come easily. I've wrestled with the pressure to "boil the ocean" to achieve financial freedom and professional success while raising daughters who are increasingly independent. My own dreams constantly shift, but in these moments, I reflect on what truly matters: my girls are my legacy. The sacrifices I've made, the hours spent guiding them, supporting them, and creating opportunities for them, are the most meaningful investments of my life.

The biggest challenges often come from my own expectations and fears. Dave's willingness to give the girls more freedom, allowing them to explore further from home, initially clashed with my protective instincts. I worried about their safety, about letting go. But I learned to take his lead, to trust that granting independence is a necessary part of their growth. Watching them make decisions, sometimes mistakes, sometimes triumphs, has been both a mirror and a teacher. Letting go has been a form of healing, showing me that love is often an act of restraint and trust.

Daily life has shifted into a rhythm of independence and connection. Mornings are a mix of coordination and presence: dropping Kierslin at the train station for school, picking up Merhye after late rehearsals or sports practices. Yet even with packed schedules, we find ways to connect. Family moments, watching a random movie or series, playing cards, visiting events like the Pumpkin Inferno on a late Thanksgiving night, or going to the gym together, remind me that even ordinary routines can become extraordinary when shared. Sometimes it's all three of us, sometimes just one, but each moment is a thread in the fabric of our family life.

The girls' independence also brings new challenges and reflections for me. Kierslin has a boyfriend now, and navigating her romantic life has required patience and trust. Merhye prefers to dedicate more time to her extracurriculars, from sports to theatre to vocal training. The balance between their social lives, ambitions, and family time has demanded flexibility and adaptability from me. I've had to accept that the quiet moments, the shared movies, late-night chats, or random gym sessions, are as important as the grand milestones.

Even in these teen years, both girls remain remarkably disciplined. Merhye stays at the top of her class, and Kierslin maintains strong grades while pursuing her science interests. Their work at the grocery store, earning money since age fourteen, has taught them responsibility and independence. They pay for anything that is not essential, giving them a sense of ownership over their lives. Watching them balance academics, work, extracurriculars, and friendships while still prioritizing family is one of the greatest joys of parenting I've experienced.

Healing as a parent has been an ongoing journey. I've had to confront my own desires, my fears, and my need for control. I've learned that my daughters' independence is not a loss but a reflection of the love, discipline, and values I've instilled. It forces me to look inward and consider who I am outside of motherhood. The less they need me, the more I am challenged to find my own purpose, my own passions, and my own voice.

The small moments remain the most profound. Driving Kierslin to the train station, picking up Merhye after rehearsal, laughing over a random card game, or marveling at Merhye's progress with her vocal coach, these ordinary experiences are the building blocks of family, love, and personal growth. They remind me that healing doesn't happen in grand gestures, but in presence, patience, and reflection.

I have come to see that my greatest accomplishments are my daughters; their discipline, independence, kindness, and ambition are the fruits of the love and guidance I've poured into them. My role as their mother is not to control or dictate their lives but to support, guide, and witness their journey.

In doing so, I continue to heal, growing alongside them while discovering my own identity in the process.

Parenting teenagers is not without its challenges, periods, hormones, dating, and the occasional disagreement, but the lessons are profound. Discipline was unnecessary because they internalized it from years of guidance, love, and routine. Acts of service, whether feeding the homeless or helping others in need, keep them grounded and humble. Watching them navigate life with grace, independence, and empathy is the clearest reflection of what parenting and healing truly mean: love, presence, and letting go.

✦ Reflection & Takeaway ✦

Parenting teens is a mirror reflecting not only who they are becoming, but who you are becoming alongside them.

Their growing independence challenges you to let go, to trust, and to redefine your identity beyond motherhood in the quiet routines, the late-night chats, and the shared laughter. You discover that your greatest successes are not measured in accolades or achievements, but in the love, discipline, and values you have nurtured.

Pause & Consider

How does your children's independence challenge you to discover or reclaim your own identity?

In what ways can letting go be an act of love and healing for both you and your children?

How do everyday moments like riding to school, card games, or shared gym sessions shape your sense of purpose, connection, and growth as a parent?

Chapter 13: The Balance of Becoming

There's a certain kind of quiet that enters a home once your children start living beyond your daily reach. It's not silence, not really; it's the gentle hum of change. The sound of doors opening and closing later than they used to, the creak of stairs as one of them comes home from a shift or practice, the faint echo of laughter from another room instead of the constant chatter that once filled every corner.

It's strange, this new rhythm. I used to crave moments of peace when the girls were little; a few minutes of quiet felt like gold. Now, that same quiet feels like a mirror, reflecting all the parts of myself I've put on hold.

For years, motherhood gave me my purpose. My days were full, sometimes too full, but always meaningful. Every meal cooked, every school project supervised, every bedtime conversation anchored me. I was the pulse that kept our family steady. But now, with both girls more independent, I feel that same pulse slowing down. They're thriving, working, studying, chasing passions, and I couldn't be prouder. But the less they need me, the more I'm faced with the question: Who am I now?

I've been chasing financial freedom, trying on different versions of myself to see which one feels like home. I've worn so many hats I've lost count: creator, entrepreneur, dreamer, caregiver. Each one feels right for a while, and then something inside me shifts. I lose momentum, lose interest, or lose the belief that I can make it work. Then I start again, convincing myself that this time I'll finally "get there."

But lately, I've been realizing that I might be chasing something deeper than financial freedom. I'm chasing identity freedom. The ability to stand on my own, not as "Mom," or "wife," or "provider," but as me.

It's not easy to separate the two. So much of who I am has been built around nurturing others through food, through emotional care, through holding space for healing. I've always believed that motherhood and love were my strongest callings. But what happens when that calling changes shape? When nurturing others, does it no longer leave room for nurturing yourself?

Carving out time for me feels like an act of rebellion sometimes. I'll sit down to write or plan something for myself, and within minutes, my mind wanders to what still needs to be done: the laundry, the groceries, the appointments, the trivial things that always seem louder than my own needs. I start to feel like I'm neglecting something or someone. Then guilt sets in, the kind that whispers, "You don't get to rest yet; there's still more to do."

And when I do carve out time, really carve it out, I often feel lost in it. Like I've been swimming so long in everyone else's currents that I no longer know where my own shoreline is. That's when the fear creeps in, not just because of failure, but of solitude, of realizing that I'm not entirely sure who I am when no one asks me.

I've learned that being afraid to be alone isn't about not wanting solitude; it's about not knowing what to do with it. For years, my self-worth came from being needed, from keeping things running smoothly, from being the dependable one. Now, I must learn to need myself in that same way; to show up for me with the same consistency and care I've given everyone else.

And then there's my marriage. Dave and I have built a life together through every imaginable season: the chaos of early parenthood, the exhaustion of working and raising kids, the slow unfolding of midlife. But now, as we both start looking toward our next chapters, I realize we're standing at different crossroads. He's content with the stillness; I'm restless in it. He's settled into routine; I'm craving something more. It's not that love has disappeared; it's that it's asking to evolve.

We've had to relearn what partnership means in this stage. Some days, we find our rhythm easily, laughing in the kitchen, teasing each other like teenagers, planning the next weekend adventure. Other days, we speak different languages. It's hard to admit that even after so many years, connections take effort. It's not a given; it's a choice you keep making.

I sometimes look at him and wonder, how do we reinvent something that's already so familiar? How do we find new ways to grow together when our dreams no longer look the same? There's no map for this kind of navigation. You just keep walking, hoping the road ahead still meets in the middle.

I've realized that balance isn't about doing everything at once. It's about knowing when to set something down. It's learning to trust that even if I don't have every dream figured out, I'm still moving forward. It's accepting that motherhood, marriage, and self-discovery will always overlap, sometimes gracefully, sometimes messily, and that's okay.

When I think about my girls, their courage, their creativity, their drive, I see pieces of me in them. That's my legacy, my success story. Not the business I've yet to build or the project I've yet to finish, but the two incredible humans who carry my lessons forward in their own ways. I poured my energy into shaping them, but what I didn't realize was how much they were shaping me in return.

As Merhye chases her dreams of music and performance, I see the same spark I had when I auditioned for Canadian Idol and La Voix. It's poetic, really, the same man, Farley Flex, who once watched my younger self sing, now witnessing my daughter take her shot. It feels like life has come full circle, reminding me that even dreams you let go of have a way of resurfacing through the next generation.

But I've made peace with that. I'm not trying to live through her or rewrite my own story through hers. I'm simply grateful to have been part of her journey, to be close enough to witness her finding her voice while I'm learning to rediscover mine.

I think the lesson in all of this is that becoming doesn't stop. You don't grow up once; you grow up again. Motherhood, love, and ambition, they all stretch and shift as you do. I used to think I'd eventually land in a version of myself that felt complete. Now, I know there's no finish line. There's only the quiet, beautiful work of showing up for your family, for your dreams, and for the person you're still becoming.

That's what balance really is: Learning to hold both giving and the growing, the chaos and the calm, and realizing that neither takes away from the other. They coexist, constantly shaping each other.

And this stage, this messy, beautiful middle, isn't about finding balance at all. It's about learning to be balanced.

✦ **Reflection & Takeaway** ✦

There comes a time in every mother's life when the house grows quieter, and the mirror starts asking new questions. Who am I when no one needs me right now? What do I dream of when I'm not dreaming for someone else?

This chapter is about that tender space in between the slow rediscovery of self, while still being the anchor for everyone you love. You've spent years building stability for others; now it's time to extend that same care inward.

Healing in this season isn't loud or dramatic; it's steady, deliberate, and deeply personal. It's learning to sit in the silence without rushing to fill it. It's trusting that your worth isn't measured by how much you do for others but by how fully you allow yourself to be.

The balance you're seeking may never look perfect, but it will feel truer each time you choose presence over perfection, curiosity over comparison, and self-trust over self-doubt.

Pause & Consider

When the noise of responsibility quiets, what parts of yourself are waiting to be heard?

How can you pursue your own dreams without losing the deep connection that motherhood brings?

In what ways can you invite your partner, or yourself, into a new kind of growth that honors who you both are now?

What would balance look like if it meant wholeness, not busyness?

Chapter 14: Reclaiming Myself

There comes a time in every mother's life when the noise quiets, when the chaos that once filled every corner of the house fades into a hum. For years, my identity was woven into motherhood, every breath timed around someone else's needs, every moment measured by their milestones. But lately, as the girls have grown more independent, I've started to hear something different: The sound of my own thoughts asking softly, "Now what?"

For so long, I defined myself by their schedules, their dreams, their laughter. My days revolved around who they were becoming. But somewhere in that process, I stopped tending to who I was becoming. As they moved toward independence, I began to realize that my healing wasn't about recovering from the past; it was also about rediscovering who I am beyond motherhood.

I've always been a woman of many hats. I worked in Corporate America, flying all over the U.S., walking into rooms that made me feel powerful and small at the same time. Then came entrepreneurship: a call center, a residential and commercial cleaning business, countless projects that challenged and stretched me. Now, again, I work as a Special

Education Tech, which fills me with a sense of purpose that no title ever could. But through it all, I've learned that not every chapter of life is about climbing. Some are about grounding.

Cooking has always been that grounding space for me. There's something sacred about chopping vegetables, stirring sauces, and bringing people together over food. In the kitchen, I feel both creative and at peace. It's one of the few places where I don't question myself. It's why I started doing content videos on meal planning, running an e-commerce business, and even launching a podcast. None of them has taken off in the way I might have dreamed, but each one has taught me something about who I am and what lights me up. I used to label them as failures, but now I see them as reminders that passion doesn't always need profit to be worthwhile.

I've realized I chased many dreams because I haven't yet found the one that fits. I'm still looking for that intersection where purpose meets peace. But if I had to guess, it's somewhere between motherhood and food, creation, and care, somewhere that feels like home.

My volunteer work at school, especially helping with musical theatre, gives me that same spark. Watching kids step into their power on stage, helping them find their voice, reminds me of something I once loved too: Performing, expressing, singing. I see a part of myself in those students, just like I see it in Merhye. When she sings, I feel every note deep in my bones. It brings me back to when I auditioned, trembling but full of hope. I still remember standing in front of the judges, never realizing that years later, my daughter would audition for one of the same during CMTC, the moment that connected her to her production company. Watching her in that space made me emotional. It felt like the universe was reminding me that my dreams didn't die; they evolved through her.

Still, I'm learning to separate my dreams from hers. I've had to make peace with the part of me that still craves success, that still wants to "make it." I've had to be careful not to project that onto her. I want her to rise because it's her calling, not because I once stood on a similar path. She deserves to fly freely, without the weight of my unfinished ambitions on her wings.

But that doesn't mean I've stopped dreaming. I'm still chasing my version of financial freedom, still trying to find that one thing that feels right. The challenge is, every time I think I've found it, another idea pulls me in. I start projects, I juggle too much, and then I burn out. I convince myself I'm wasting time because I haven't "figured it out" when in truth, I'm learning, sometimes the hard way, that figuring it out is the process.

One of my biggest lessons has been realizing that I don't always finish things because I'm scared to fail. If I don't see something through, then I can tell myself it wasn't the right fit, rather than admitting I was afraid it wouldn't work. It's a pattern I'm trying to break, one small habit at a time.

At the heart of it, my biggest fear isn't failure; it's being alone. When the girls eventually move out, I'll have to face the silence I used to crave. I'll have to redefine what "home" feels like when it's no longer full of noise and constant motion. It's both beautiful and terrifying.

Marriage has been another part of that reckoning. Dave and I have built a life that's solid, steady, dependable, loving in its own quiet way, but often lacking in the connection that once came so easily. We coexist peacefully most days, orbiting each other with familiarity rather than fire. Sometimes, I miss the spark. I miss the version of us that used to laugh until we cried, the one that went dancing until sunrise, the one that couldn't keep their hands off each other.

Now, we try. We go away on trips, have our date nights, and find moments of fun. But there's still a distance across which I can't quite reach. Dave doesn't speak my love language, and while I've accepted that he loves me in his own way, part of me still aches for words, affection, and emotional connection. He's often tired, quiet, and withdrawn, while I'm bursting with energy, conversation, and ideas. I'm the extrovert who craves expression; he's the introvert who craves calmness. It's dynamic that works until it doesn't.

And yet, when I step back, I see that we've survived storms before. This isn't the end of something; it's a transition. This is where we learn to love each other differently, where we stop trying to recapture who we were and instead learn to embrace who we are now. Relationships evolve just like people do. Ours is waiting for its next version.

These days, I'm learning to schedule time for myself the way I once scheduled time for everyone else. I'm rediscovering the joy of solo travel, the peace of writing, and the healing power of this very book. Writing has been like holding up a mirror, forcing me to see the parts I've ignored, to make peace with both the woman I've been and the one I'm still becoming.

And through it all, I sing again. Not for an audience this time, but for myself. Sometimes in the kitchen while cooking dinner, sometimes in the car on my way to work. My voice, once hidden beneath the weight of responsibility, feels free again.

I'm proud of my daughters, of their ambition, discipline, kindness, and drive. They're proof that I've done something right. But I'm also learning that I still deserve to dream for myself, not just through them.

Healing, I've learned, isn't about going backward; it's about becoming whole again, piece by piece. Maybe reclaiming myself doesn't mean returning to who I was before motherhood. It means embracing who I've grown into because of it, the woman who raised strong daughters, chased dreams, loved deeply, and is still brave enough to keep reinventing herself.

✦ **Reflection & Takeaway** ✦

Healing doesn't always come as a single revelation; it often arrives quietly, through the ordinary moments when you stop to notice yourself again. The journey of reclaiming who you are beyond motherhood is not about letting go of your children or your family; it's about returning home to your own soul.

As your world shifts and your roles evolve, the challenge becomes learning to hold both the love that pours outward and the self that still longs to grow inward. It's not selfish to seek your purpose again. It's sacred.

You are allowed to keep dreaming. You are allowed to reinvent yourself. You are allowed to shine, even as you cheer for everyone else's light.

Pause & Consider

How often do you give yourself permission to explore who you are outside of motherhood or partnership?

What creative spaces, passions, or callings make you feel most alive, and how can you nurture them more intentionally?

Are there areas in your relationship or daily life where you've settled for comfort instead of connection?

What does "reclaiming yourself" look like in this season of your life, and what small steps can you take today to honor yourself?

How can you remind yourself that your worth isn't tied to productivity or perfection, but to presence and authenticity?

Chapter 15: The Art of Letting Go & Growing

As the girls grow older, I've come to realize that parenting isn't about guiding them; it's about learning to let go while still holding space for them, and in the process, discovering the freedom to grow myself. Merhye and Kierslin's increasing independence has forced me to confront my own fears, my need for control, and the limitations I've placed on myself. It's been a journey of trust, patience, and sometimes discomfort, but one that has revealed profound lessons in both parenting and personal growth.

Merhye, now fourteen, occasionally wants to stay at friends' houses, even once for two nights in a row. This doesn't happen often, but when it does, I've learned to be okay with it. Initially, this was difficult for me. I worried endlessly about what might happen, imagining all the "what ifs" that could go wrong. Yet, over time, I noticed that Merhye approaches these experiences with a thoughtfulness and responsibility that surprises me. She tells me about the disappointment she feels when friends make poor choices, stealing, drinking, or behaving unkindly, and I see her processing these situations with empathy and maturity. Watching her navigate these experiences reinforces my trust in the values I've instilled in her. I cannot control every moment, but I can guide her toward understanding right from wrong and step back when the lessons are hers to learn.

Kierslin, at sixteen, began taking the train downtown by herself with friends. Naturally, I felt nervous, images of potential dangers flashed through my mind, and I wrestled with the fear of letting go. But I also knew that holding her back out of fear would stunt her growth. She has learned mindfulness, responsibility, and awareness of her surroundings, qualities that now shine as she moves confidently through life. Releasing the fear of the unknown has been a major step in my own healing. It's taught me that control is an illusion and that trust, both in our children and in myself, is a powerful and necessary act of love.

This chapter of our lives has also forced me to confront challenges in my own boundaries and values. I've reached a point where I have zero tolerance for gossip, jealousy, or mean behavior. I will not allow anyone to play childish games or manipulate situations through passive aggression. If someone crosses a line, I call it out because I've learned that my energy is too precious to be wasted. This principle extends across all areas of my life, family, friends, and colleagues alike. I've had to let go of toxic relationships, including some family ties, understanding that I can no longer allow others to control or silence me. Letting go of these people has been both liberating and painful, but it's necessary for my growth and the growth of my girls.

Parenting has become a mirror in many ways. The girls notice everything. When I make a mistake, I own it openly, showing them that mistakes are not failures; they are opportunities to gain experience and evolve. I model accountability, demonstrating that it's possible to confront errors with grace and humility. In turn, the girls have learned that growth is ongoing and that self-improvement is not just a concept but a lived practice. This mutual growth has strengthened our bond, teaching all of us that vulnerability, honesty, and reflection are key components of both parenting and healing.

Letting go isn't about the girls. It's also about giving myself permission to pursue my own dreams without guilt or hesitation. I've experimented with multiple creative outlets, content videos, e-commerce, and podcasts, but none have yet brought the level of success I desire. Each project is a lesson, a reminder that failure and experimentation are part of the journey. My e-commerce venture, though still growing, is a space where I take risks, learn, and challenge myself. I've realized that the patience, resilience, and creativity I've instilled in the girls are the very qualities I must cultivate in my own life.

The daily realities of letting go are intertwined with small, concrete moments. I observe Merhye navigating complex friendships and ethical decisions, Kierslin exploring independence in the city, and myself learning to carve out time for my ambitions while still being fully present for the girls. There is a delicate balance between giving them freedom and maintaining connection. I must remind myself to celebrate their independence rather than fear it. Every new responsibility they embrace, every milestone they achieve, is a testament to the foundation I've worked so hard to build with Dave, for the girls, and for myself.

Challenges continue, as they always will. I wrestle with time management, self-care, and the fear that I am not pursuing my full potential beyond motherhood. Dave and I navigate a relationship that requires effort to maintain a connection, and sometimes our personalities clash. I am extroverted, driven, and eager for engagement, while he is more introverted and often fatigued. Finding a rhythm that accommodates both our needs and prioritizes the girls has been another exercise in letting go, compromise, and growth.

Through it all, I've discovered that letting go is not abandonment; it is trust, love, and courage. I am learning to accept that my daughters will make decisions I cannot control, that life will unfold beyond my hands, and that my own identity is still being shaped even as I nurture theirs. The more I release fear and control, the more I uncover the joy of watching them grow into thoughtful, compassionate, and capable young women.

Parenting teenage children has taught me to embrace paradoxes: freedom and boundaries coexist, love and letting go coexist, and healing comes in the form of trust. It is trust in them, in myself, and in the natural unfolding of life. By stepping back, I allow the girls to navigate their own paths, and in doing so, I step forward on my own. In that shared growth lies resilience, courage, and the ongoing art of letting go, a lesson that will continue to shape our lives for years to come.

✦ Reflection & Takeaway ✦

Letting go is not about losing control; it's about creating space for trust, growth, and freedom. As your children gain independence, you discover your own resilience, your own boundaries, and the courage to face the unknown. Growth is not linear, and parenting older children reflects that truth in the most profound ways.

Pause & Consider

In what areas of your life do you need to release control to allow growth, for yourself and those you love?

How can modeling accountability and reflection inspire the next generation to navigate challenges with integrity?

What lessons of trust, resilience, and courage can you embrace as you balance supporting others and nurturing your own path?

Chapter 16: Parenting Without Perfection

As my girls continue to grow into independent young women, I've come to realize that parenting is not about having all the answers or doing everything flawlessly. Every decision I make, big or small, carries weight, but none of them is perfect, and that's okay. In fact, it's within imperfections that the most important lessons unfold, both for them and for me.

I've learned to embrace mistakes as opportunities to model growth. When Merhye calls me out on something I've done wrong, I don't deflect or make excuses. I own it. I show her that it's possible to make an error, face it, and learn from it. Kierslin sees it too, and in these moments, I'm teaching both that resilience, accountability, and humility are far more valuable than perfection.

Letting go of the need to control every outcome has been one of the hardest, yet most freeing, parts of raising teenagers. Merhye occasionally wants to stay at friends' houses for more than one night, and I've had to trust her judgment, even when my mind races with what-ifs. Kierslin navigating downtown independently at 16 forced me to confront my fears about the unknown. I couldn't let anxiety dictate my parenting; I had to trust that the values, discipline, and awareness I instilled in them would guide their decisions.

Parenting without perfection also means redefining my own expectations. I don't have to excel at everything at the same time. My attempts at content creation, my e-commerce endeavors, and even my volunteer work may not always meet my own standards, but they are part of the process of finding myself, alongside guiding my daughters. I am learning to celebrate small wins, to be patient with myself, and to understand that healing is ongoing, messy, and deeply personal.

I have made mistakes. I forget things and sometimes get mad over nonsense because my mood shifts. I overindulged and got drunk to the point of forgetting what happened a few times, and my girls were around. One time, I stupidly accepted a shot from a stranger at a bar, a moment I cringe to remember, yet it taught me to be mindful and cautious. I have made promises I didn't keep. I have spoken poorly to their father when I was upset, even in their presence. And yes, there are moments of tension, frustration, and regret, but there are also moments of laughter, where the girls and I laugh at my mistakes, like when I say the wrong thing or mispronounce something absurd. These imperfect, human moments are teaching them and reminding me that life is lived in shades of grey, not in absolutes.

By being imperfect, Dave and I have learned to accept each other's flaws. We've had our own moments of miscommunication, frustration, and silent tension, yet we've grown in how we navigate each other's moods. I've let go of caring what others think, and I no longer feel obligated to maintain relationships with people who are cruel or toxic just because they are family. The boundaries I've set are not just for my own sanity; they are lessons for my girls on self-respect, courage, and choosing your battles wisely.

Even amid chaos, ordinary moments are powerful. When I get frustrated or lose my temper over trivial things, it becomes a teaching moment about emotions. When I slip up or misstep, the girls see me manage it, apologize, and move forward. These daily demonstrations of imperfection teach them that growth isn't about avoiding mistakes; it's about how we respond to them.

Parenting without perfection also means letting go of control. I can't dictate every decision, every social outing, or every choice my girls make, but I can guide them with love, wisdom, and presence. I've had to trust that Merhye and Kierslin will make choices rooted in the values we've instilled: honesty, kindness, discipline, and accountability. Watching them navigate independence, sometimes confidently and sometimes clumsily, reminds me that my role is not to shield them from mistakes but to equip them with the tools to manage them.

In this imperfection, I have also discovered freedom. I am free to explore my own dreams without guilt, free to pursue passions like content creation, cooking, volunteering, and singing, and free to reinvent my marriage alongside a partner who is also learning to accept himself. The girls' independence allows me to reclaim my time while remaining present, creating a rhythm of balance between mothering and self-discovery.

The lessons extend beyond parenting. Owning my mistakes, embracing imperfection, and letting go of unhealthy expectations have reshaped how I navigate all relationships. I no longer tolerate gossip, passive aggression, or people who drain me emotionally. I've learned to speak my truth, assert boundaries, and let go of what doesn't serve me, lessons that ripple into the way I teach my daughters to approach life.

Parenting without perfection doesn't mean I am careless or indifferent; it means I am human, present, and mindful. It's about showing my daughters that life will not always be smooth, that we will stumble, falter, and make questionable decisions, but that growth, accountability, and love are what truly matter. I hope that by watching me navigate my own imperfection, they will internalize the courage to face their own challenges, take risks, and accept themselves fully.

The truth is that perfection is an illusion. Parenting is not about flawless execution; it's about showing up, learning, healing, and growing alongside your children. And in embracing my own imperfections, I've discovered a deeper connection to my daughters, a clearer vision of myself, and a quiet but powerful joy in knowing that the legacy I am leaving them is one of resilience, authenticity, and unconditional love.

✦ Reflection & Takeaway ✦

Healing and growth do not require perfection; they require presence, accountability, and courage. By showing your children how to navigate mistakes, emotions, and challenges, you teach them resilience and self-awareness. Imperfection becomes a mirror for growth, both for you and for those you love most.

Pause & Consider

How does embracing your own mistakes model resilience and accountability for your children?

In what ways can letting go of control and perfection open space for trust, independence, and growth?

How can imperfection become a source of connection, authenticity, and healing in your relationships?

Chapter 17: The Grace of Imperfection

Healing doesn't always come as a grand revelation. Sometimes it arrives quietly, tucked between an exhale and a moment of stillness, when you finally stop fighting yourself and start listening.

For years, I tried to be the perfect mother, wife, woman, and provider. I wanted everything I did to prove that I had broken the cycle I grew up in, that I could create peace where there had once been chaos. But perfection is heavy. It breaks you quietly. What I've learned instead is that grace, real, gentle, forgiving grace, is what heals.

I made a choice long ago that I would never spank my girls. I knew the kind of hurt that grows from fear and how it shapes you long after the bruises fade. The one-time Dave spanked one of them, out of anger, but I didn't yell. I just told him softly but firmly that it could never happen again. I told him what that did to me as a child, how it made me question love and safety. He understood, truly. That moment changed him, and it reminded me that healing doesn't just live in forgiveness; it also lives in the courage to speak your truth without rage.

There are parts of me I used to be ashamed of. Two times I drank too much, forgetting pieces of the night and waking up with regret. Times I accepted a drink from a stranger and realized later how reckless it was. Moments when I spoke too harshly about Dave in front of the girls, allowing anger to spill into the space where love should have been. I've made promises I didn't keep. I've reacted before thinking. But every one of those moments has been a lesson, an opportunity to gain experience.

The beauty of motherhood, I've learned, is that it humbles you. My girls have called me out more than once for saying something I shouldn't have or acting out of frustration. And every time, I take it. I listen. I own it. Because I want them to see that strength doesn't mean pretending to be perfect. It means having the courage to admit when you've failed and then standing back up with grace.

They've seen me laugh at myself, too, the silly mistakes, the wrong words, the times I completely miss the mark. And we laugh together. Those moments remind me that love doesn't demand perfection; it thrives in honesty.

Cooking has always been my peace. There's something about the rhythm of chopping, stirring, and seasoning that brings me back to myself. When I'm in the kitchen, music playing and the smell of food filling the air, I feel centered. I share my cooking online, videos, recipes, and a little glimpse of joy. It's not wildly successful, but it's mine. It's real. It's love expressed through food.

I walk, I dance, I sing, all parts of my self-care that bring me calm. My podcast room is my sacred space, where I write, record, and reflect. It's the one place that's entirely mine, filled with the sound of my own voice and the stories I've lived through. I find clarity there. It's where I realize that healing isn't about reinventing yourself; it's about remembering who you were before the world told you who to be.

I used to give too much of myself to everyone else, saying yes when I was exhausted, showing up when I was empty, mistaking overextending for love. I finally forgave myself when I stopped doing that. It happened when I started loving myself as fiercely as I love others. That shift didn't happen overnight; it came in pieces. But it came.

Now, I have no patience for cruelty or gossip. I won't let someone's jealousy or bitterness live rent-free in my mind. The noise of the world, ugliness, and small-mindedness used to consume me. Now I let it pass. I've cut ties with family members who refuse to treat me with respect, and though it hurt, it was freedom disguised as loss. Protecting my peace is an act of healing, not rebellion.

There are still days when I get angry over trivial things, when my emotions shift before I can catch them. I've learned to pause, to breathe, to not let the storm win. Healing hasn't made me perfect; it's made me aware. I talk through my stress instead of burying it. I laugh more. I cry when I need to. I no longer confuse emotional survival with strength.

The girls see that, too. They see a woman who has stumbled but stands taller for it. They tease me when I forget things, poke fun when I mispronounce a word, and laugh when I make a mess of something simple. But beneath it all, there's love and respect, an unspoken knowing that we've built something solid together.

There's a moment every year that brings it all into focus, me in the kitchen during Thanksgiving or Christmas, the smell of food swirling through the house while the girls are somewhere nearby, talking, laughing, living. It's in those quiet, ordinary moments that I feel closest to peace. Gratitude fills the spaces where guilt used to live.

Because I know now that I don't need to be everything, I just need to be.

And in being flawed, growing, forgiving, I am enough.

Healing is not the end of the story. It's the bridge between who I was and who I am becoming. And that's what grace really is, the soft place between the breaking and the becoming, the quiet truth that love, in all its imperfect forms, was never lost. It was just waiting for me to come home to it.

Some days I still question where I am headed, whether my e-commerce dreams will ever take off, and whether I'll find the balance between passion and peace. But I've come to understand that success looks different when your heart has healed a little. It's not measured in numbers, followers, or recognition. It's found in the laughter at the dinner table, the long drives with my girls singing along to our favorite songs, the small moments of stillness where I feel gratitude wash over me like sunlight.

The version of me who used to chase perfection wouldn't recognize this woman, softer, but stronger. She'd wonder how I can be content while still wanting more. But that's the gift of healing: it teaches you that both can coexist. You can crave growth without self-loathing. You can still reach for dreams while staying grounded in love.

Some nights I sit in the quiet and talk to my younger self, the scared little girl who wanted to be seen, who thought she had to earn love by being good. I tell her she did the best she could. I tell her we made it. And in that conversation, I feel peace. True, unshakable peace.

Healing has made me realize that I don't need to have it all figured out to live beautifully. I just need to keep showing up for myself, for my girls, for the love that keeps growing through every imperfection.

✦ **Reflection & Takeaway** ✦

Healing doesn't erase the past; it transforms how you carry it. Through mistakes, laughter, and forgiveness, we learn that grace isn't about perfection but presence. By allowing ourselves to be vulnerable, we teach those we love that growth is not about never falling but about rising differently each time.

Pause & Consider

How can you show yourself more grace when you make mistakes?

In what ways do your imperfections make you more relatable, more human, and more whole?

What moments of laughter, humility, or truth have become part of your healing journey?

Who would you be if you stopped trying to be everything to everyone and simply allowed yourself to be?

Chapter 18: Rediscovering Joy & Purpose

There's a quietness that has started to live inside me now, a peace I never used to know. It doesn't mean life is calm all the time, but I no longer carry the same weight of trying to prove myself to everyone. I've learned to let people's noise stay where it belongs, with them. The world keeps testing me, of course. There are moments when the ugliness of others creeps in, small-minded people with cruel intentions who want to stir up drama and drag me into it. I no longer entertain it. My tolerance for meanness and manipulation has all but disappeared. I've spent too much of my life trying to be the bigger person in rooms full of people who weren't even trying to grow. Now, I simply walk away.

The peace I have now didn't appear overnight; it came from years of chaos, reflection, and learning to hold myself accountable. When my girls call me out on something I've done wrong, I don't shrink from it. I own it. I show them what it looks like to face a mistake without excuses, because I want them to see that strength isn't perfect; it's humility. They tease me sometimes, poking fun at the moments when I say the wrong thing or forget something small, but beneath it all, there's respect. They know I'm not afraid to admit when I've fallen short, and that's something I never had the courage to do as a child.

Every day feels like a test of balance between letting go and holding on, between supporting my daughters and rediscovering myself. Watching them move through the world with confidence and independence brings me more joy than anything I've ever done. I see myself in them, the strength, the curiosity, the empathy, but I also see the difference. They've grown up in love and security, and that has given them wings I never had. Seeing them balance work, extracurriculars, relationships, and school with such grace reminds me that I've done something right.

Still, there are moments when the world tries to pull me backward. There are people who feed off negativity, who use gossip and intimidation as tools, and I can feel the tug of old habits to defend, to explain, to make peace. But I don't. Not anymore. I've come to realize that peace doesn't mean silence. It means knowing when to speak truth and when to walk away. The more I heal, the less I tolerate cruelty, and the faster I can let go of what doesn't align with the woman I'm becoming.

My healing lives in motion. Long walks clear my mind, the rhythm of my steps synchronizing with the beat of my favorite songs. Jogging helps me process the noise in my head, burning away frustration and replacing it with calm. Music lifts me in ways nothing else can; sometimes I sing aloud, sometimes I just listen. Either way, those moments feel sacred. They remind me that joy doesn't have to be loud or extravagant; it can live in the quiet moments between chaos and calm.

Cooking remains one of my greatest forms of therapy. There's something grounding about being in the kitchen, the smell of garlic and onions, the rhythm of chopping, the warmth that fills the space. It brings me peace, connects me to the best parts of myself, and often becomes the backdrop of our family's laughter. The girls will wander in and out, stealing bites or offering opinions. Those moments, simple as they are, hold me together. They remind me that success isn't about money or fame; it's about creating spaces where love lives, and laughter echoes.

I used to think success meant having my name known, my voice heard by thousands, or my bank account overflowing. I chased dreams of fame and recognition, believing that validation lived outside of me. Now, I see success in smaller, deeper things. It's in the discipline of writing that I'd rather rest. It's in creating content that feeds my passions instead of my ego. It's in the laughter that fills the house, the calm that follows a storm, and the way I can sit alone now without feeling lonely.

I'm still soul-searching, but it no longer feels desperate. It feels like an adventure, one where I get to redefine what happiness looks like on my own terms. I'm discovering that peace isn't something you find once and keep; it's something you choose repeatedly. Each day, I decide what kind of energy I'll allow in and what kind I'll release. I choose gratitude, even when the world feels hard. I remind myself that the things testing me are also teaching me, that even when people are cruel or situations unfair, I can remain kind without being a pushover.

Laughter continues to be medicine. Sometimes, it's over nothing at all, just me and the girls laughing at something silly I said or a story that takes a turn we didn't expect. Other times, it's deep, healing laughter that comes after tears, the kind that reminds me how far we've come as a family. Those moments are sacred. They are proof that we've built something real, something strong enough to hold both pain and joy.

I've stopped giving every piece of myself away. That might be the clearest sign of healing. I no longer need to pour from an empty cup to feel useful or loved. I know my worth now, and I protect my peace like it's gold. I'm not afraid to cut ties with those who are toxic or cruel, even if they share my blood. Love without respect isn't love; it's control. And I've learned I don't owe anyone my silence in the name of keeping peace.

Now, I fill my life with what brings me light. Writing. Singing. Cooking. Laughing. Moving my body. These things reconnect me to who I am beyond motherhood, beyond pain, beyond the expectations of others. Healing has made me softer in some ways and stronger in others. I've become more patient, but also more assertive. I know what I need now, and I'm not afraid to say it.

Peace, for me, isn't about everything being perfect; it's about knowing I can manage it when it's not.

✦ **Reflection & Takeaway** ✦

Peace doesn't always come from silence; it often arrives in the middle of noise, through the moments we choose to stand tall instead of shrinking, to laugh instead of breaking, to let go instead of holding on too tightly.

Pause & Consider

What small, daily rituals bring you peace and clarity?

When was the last time you redefined what success means to you?

How can you protect your peace without closing your heart?

In what ways has letting go opened space for new joy and self-discovery?

Chapter 19: The Woman Beneath the Roles

Healing has a way of stripping you down, not to break you, but to finally reveal you. For so long, my identity lived inside the roles I played: daughter, sister, wife, mother, protector. It was easy to hide behind those labels, to let them define me, to assume they were all I was meant to be. But somewhere along this journey, I started feeling something deeper trying to surface, the woman beneath the roles, the version of me I never had time to meet.

I have always been empathetic, resilient, protective, and loyal. Those qualities showed up even as a child, long before adulthood placed titles on my shoulders. As I grew, I became emotionally insightful, creative, expressive, analytical, and overwhelmingly driven, even on the days when I felt like life was determined to drown me. But I didn't always know how to name or value these parts of myself. For most of my life, my worth was something I measured through survival, through what I endured, not through who I was.

I was once a free spirit who stopped for anyone and everyone who needed help. I offered my heart like an open door. I didn't care about boundaries or limits; I just cared about people. Before motherhood, I would leap into the world with no fear of breaking, because I was already used to being broken. Helping others made me feel needed and purposeful, even if it cost me pieces of myself; I couldn't afford to lose.

Motherhood changed that. Motherhood made me fierce. Protective in a way that surprised even me. Emotionally insightful in ways I had never been before. And suddenly the world felt sharper, heavier, more dangerous, not just for me, but to the little souls I was now responsible for. The wildness in me quieted, shifting into something more grounded. I learned to question who deserved space in my life. And for the first time ever, I began asking myself a question I had never considered: What about me?

Cooking came into my life as a necessity, but stayed as a passion. Before the girls, I cooked only out of obligation. But after becoming a mother, something shifted. Cooking became therapeutic, a way to love, to nurture, to create beauty from simple things. I started developing a palate I didn't even know I had, tasting flavors as metaphors for life: the sweetness, the heat, the bitterness, the unexpected harmony of it all. Sharing that cooking content on social media became another surprising form of connection, another outlet to create and express. I never imagined food would be a chapter in my healing, but life always hides remedies in the most ordinary places.

Music, singing, and dancing have always been my emotional release, my unfiltered truth. When I sing, I feel everything. I don't always have the words to say. When I dance, I shake loose the pain that tries to settle in my bones. When I listen to music, I hear pieces of myself in every lyric. And when I walk or jog, healing moves through me, healing in motion, like the universe reminding me that staying still is not the only way to recover.

My podcast room became my sanctuary, the place where my thoughts untangle, where my truth travels from my chest to my voice without fear of interruption. It's where I think best, where I write, where I speak my truth aloud. Creating my podcast started as something for others, but eventually I realized it was for me. My voice had spent so many years silenced, dismissed, or punished; no wonder it needed a room of its own to breathe.

This book is part of that same unfolding. A place to place the pieces. A way to trace the line of my healing so others can find theirs. A way to break generational silence by naming what tried to destroy me, and equally naming everything I have become despite it all.

And yet, with all this growth, life still tests me. The world is full of mean girls, women who weaponize insecurity, who poke and prod at others because they cannot face themselves. I have far less tolerance for that nonsense now. I used to absorb other people's poor behavior as if it were my responsibility to understand or fix it. Now, I simply see it for what it is: a reflection of their pain, not mine. I'm still soul-searching, still unfolding, still figuring out how to navigate a world that isn't always kind. But for the first time, I'm enjoying the ride of discovering myself rather than fearing what I might find.

Seeing my girls balance their lives, make good choices, and grow into thoughtful, self-aware young women brings me joy I can't even measure. They are proof that healing does ripple forward, that cycles really can be broken. They appreciate my vulnerability, even tease me with playful jabs when I own my mistakes. Their laughter, their honesty, and their quick-witted jokes remind me that healing doesn't always come through tears. Sometimes it comes through humor, through shared stories, through the simple joy of not taking ourselves too seriously.

I've also learned that stress dissolves faster when I talk it through. Silence used to be my shield. Now, my voice is my tool. The tolerance I once had for mistreatment has faded, replaced with self-respect, boundaries, and clarity. Healing has stretched my spirit closer to what feels like a spiritual awakening, an understanding of myself that feels deeper than anything I've ever known.

My relationships with my now-estranged family members were wounds I carried for years. Wanting a bond with them, grieving the versions of them I wished existed. Those relationships were toxic, and acknowledging that truth was its own kind of heartbreak. But now, I can feel the healing finally settling in. I no longer cling to what could have been. I accept what it is, and I release what never will be.

Marriage is its own complex landscape. There are moments I feel lonely inside it, moments when the silence between us feels louder than any argument we've ever had. And then there are times when I feel like I am everything to one person, completely seen, cherished, and valued. My independence does dim at times; my voice softens when I wish it would roar. But my sense of adventure grows inside this marriage too, like a spark that refuses to die. Healing has taught me that two truths can coexist: love can be beautiful and heavy, fulfilling, and challenging. And the part that excites me most is the possibility of falling in love with my husband again, in a new way, with new eyes and a stronger version of myself.

I'm also unlearning the reactiveness and anger that hurt carved into me. Those instincts came from survival, but I'm not surviving anymore; I'm living. I'm trying to understand what I want for the rest of my life once my girls are grown up and building worlds of their own. I want financial freedom, not for luxury or status, but to help those in need and to simply live without fear of scarcity. I want success that comes from feeding my passions, not chasing old definitions of fame or money.

I'm not afraid of becoming my parents. That fear has dissolved. I am not destined to follow their path. I know now that I'm capable of building a life that is self-sufficient, grounded, and intentional. A life that influences others to heal their brokenness and become the good in the world.

My ideal life has a powerful sense of community, with relationships that are long-lasting and fruitful. I want depth, not something disposable. I want a connection that feels safe, sacred, and real.

And the most surprising part of all this?

I truly believe I deserve it.

For the first time in my life, I believe I deserve the life I am trying to build.

Now I'm simply figuring out how to get there.

✦ Reflection & Takeaway ✦

Identity is not something we find all at once; it reveals itself gently, in layers, as we heal, forgive, and choose ourselves again. In naming your gifts, your wounds, and your hopes, you reclaim the parts of you that were silenced, overlooked, or buried for survival.

This chapter is a reminder that becoming is not a destination; it's a return. A return to empathy, creativity, resilience, and truth. A return to the voice you once softened. A return to the woman who is learning to want more, deserve more, and expect more from her own life.

Pause & Consider

Which parts of your identity feel newly awakened or finally acknowledged?

How does naming your strengths change the way you move through the world?

What old patterns or wounds are you releasing to make space for your next chapter?

When you imagine your future self, emotionally free, financially secure, and creatively fulfilled, what do you look like, sound like, and feel like?

Chapter 20: Reclaiming Joy

I have learned that joy isn't something that waits for permission. It doesn't come neatly, packaged in free time or perfect conditions. It is something you take, something you carve out for yourself, even amid responsibilities, chaos, and expectations. Motherhood taught me this in ways I never could have anticipated: the art of giving everything yet still remembering to return a piece to yourself.

Singing has always been my sanctuary. I think back to my sister's wedding, before I had kids, when I stood in front of the crowd and sang a shared anthem of surviving and holding on, a gentle reminder that love was always possible. As I sang her into womanhood, a quiet celebration of everything we had endured and everything we were stepping into, adulthood, motherhood, life in all its messy beauty. That moment taught me that expression, in its purest form, is a healing act.

Even now, joy comes to me in moments that feel small to others, but monumental to me. This past Friday, with a rare day off, I spent hours baking the girls' favorite treats. Flour dusting the counter, the hum of the oven, the smell of chocolate and pumpkin filling the kitchen, it was a meditation, a ritual of love and peace. Each cookie, each cake, each perfectly imperfect cupcake was an offering of care, not just to them, but to me. I realized that nurturing is a two-way street: in nurturing them, I nurture my own soul. Baking is my way of grounding myself, of reminding myself that life is sweet even when messy.

My podcast has become another sanctuary. Recording episodes allows me to speak truths I might otherwise keep inside. Today I recorded an episode about showing grace, about managing the weight of meanness and cruelty from others, about understanding that not everyone will treat you well, and that's okay. Speaking aloud, without censor or expectation, was liberating. My voice felt like it belonged to me, fully, unapologetically. I realized that part of reclaiming joy is claiming your voice, especially when the world expects you to stay silent.

Solo travel has been transformative. My first trip alone to New York for work forced me to connect with myself in ways I had long neglected. Dining alone at a restaurant, perched at the bar, talking with strangers, observing life moving around me, I discovered a quiet confidence I hadn't allowed myself before. I realized independence doesn't mean being lonely; it means embracing your own company and finding peace in it. Even brief moments of solitude can be profoundly healing.

Creating content, experimenting with visuals, cooking videos, aesthetics, and stories, has become another outlet for my self-expression. I no longer create for approval or validation; I do it to explore, to feel, to communicate who I am without compromise. Sometimes I fear that by juggling so many projects, cooking, baking, content creation, podcasting, work, writing, and motherhood, I'm spreading myself too thin, that my inconsistencies will cost me opportunities. But I have accepted that my life, like my passions, cannot be contained in a single box. Each pursuit teaches me something new about resilience, creativity, and self-discovery.

My marriage is part of this journey as well. Dave supports me, though not always fully matching my energy or meeting me halfway, and sometimes I feel the tension of imbalance. Rather than letting it diminish my joy, I've learned to pull him into it, to model joy and enthusiasm, to remind him that life is meant to be experienced, savored, and celebrated, even amid brokenness. Our connection is sometimes subtle, a shared laugh, a spontaneous dance in the kitchen, a quiet morning together, yet these moments are precious, and they remind me that love and joy do not demand perfection.

Motherhood has become both a mirror and a compass. Watching my girls navigate their lives, seeing them balance work, school, friends, and passions, fills me with a deep sense of pride. Kierslin traveling downtown independently, Merhye making careful decisions about sleepovers and friendships, each choice reassures me that the foundation we built as parents is strong. Their independence allows me the space to reclaim pieces of myself, to experiment with who I am beyond the role of mom, yet it also keeps me grounded in what matters most: their happiness, their safety, and their growth.

Reclaiming joy has taught me to embrace imperfection. I have allowed myself to make mistakes and own them openly with the girls. I have stumbled, laughed, and sometimes cried, and in those moments, I've realized that authenticity brings a kind of peace no achievement ever could. There is quiet, unshakeable satisfaction in showing up as yourself, without pretense, for your family, your work, and yourself. My daughters witness my vulnerability and my missteps, and in doing so, they learn that imperfection is not failure; it is humanity.

I have also found joy in rhythm, literally and figuratively. Singing, dancing, cooking, walking, jogging, and creating content all allow me to move through life physically, mentally, and emotionally. There is freedom in motion, a release in expression, and a meditation in routine. Daily laughter, whether with the girls, with friends, or even with strangers, has become non-negotiable. It is medicine for the soul, a reminder that life is not only about discipline, responsibility, or achieving milestones; it is also about delight, curiosity, and connection.

Yet joy is also a lesson in patience and self-compassion. I have learned that I cannot pour from an empty cup. My efforts to "boil the ocean," to do everything and be everything, sometimes leave me exhausted, second-guessing my priorities, and questioning whether I'm choosing wisely. But even in moments of uncertainty, there is meaning. Each attempt, each experiment, each small success, or perceived failure adds texture to my journey. I am learning that joy is not a fixed destination; it is the accumulation of small, deliberate acts of presence, care, and courage.

Through all of this, I recognize that my passions, cooking, baking, singing, writing, podcasting, and independent travel, are more than hobbies. They are lifelines. They connect me to who I am beneath motherhood, beneath responsibility, beneath expectation. They are the avenues through which I process pain, celebrate life, and affirm my identity. They remind me that I am allowed to exist fully, not just in service to others, but in service to myself as well.

Reclaiming joy is also about holding space for love, for the girls, for Dave, for myself, for life. It is about practicing gratitude for small moments: the girls laughing in the kitchen, a quiet cup of coffee, a perfect song on the radio, the smell of a baking pie, and the accomplishment of a podcast episode recorded and shared. These moments are ordinary and extraordinary at once, because they remind me that life is not about grand gestures alone; it is about noticing, cherishing, and participating in the beauty around me.

Joy is the quiet courage of saying yes to yourself. It is the persistent insistence that your life is yours to shape, that love and passion can coexist with ambition, and that motherhood does not erase your identity but rather enhances it when embraced fully. I have learned that reclaiming joy is a lifelong practice, an ongoing dance between care, freedom, creativity, and self-compassion. In this dance, I am finally learning to follow my own rhythm, to trust the music of my own soul, and to let the light I carry spill into the lives of my girls, my family, and myself.

✦ **Reflection & Takeaway** ✦

Joy is not something you wait for; it is something you cultivate. It exists in the daily acts of self-expression, creativity, and care. By taking time to nurture yourself alongside those you love, you discover that self-love is not indulgent but essential.

Pause & Consider

In what ways do you actively create moments of joy for yourself, even amidst obligations?

How can expressing your passion help you heal and reconnect with your identity?

What small, consistent rituals can you adopt to nourish both your well-being and your relationships?

How might embracing joy influence the people around you and set an example for those you care about most?

Where in your life could you allow yourself to let go of fear, expectation, or guilt to fully experience your own happiness?

Chapter 21: The Woman I Am Becoming

There are seasons in a woman's life that arrive without warning, quiet shifts that don't feel like healing at first, but like exhaustion, clarity, or a sudden need to breathe differently. For me, that season began when the one person who recently tried shrinking me finally removed themselves from my life.

It was almost disorienting how quickly my energy changed.

One day, I was weighed down, doubting myself, questioning every instinct, and the next… I felt like someone had cracked open a window in a room I didn't realize had gone stale. My mind felt quieter. My laughter felt real again. There was color where things had felt gray. My joy, which had been hiding deep somewhere inside me, began rising to the surface like it had been waiting for a chance to breathe.

It made me understand something that took me decades to learn:

Some people don't leave to hurt you. They leave so you can finally hear your own voice.

For most of my life, I had been conditioned to prioritize other people's comfort before my own. As a child, I became the fixer, the peacekeeper, the emotional sponge absorbing everyone else's messes. I was the child who checked the temperature of every room before I walked into it. The child who couldn't stand to see someone upset and would sacrifice her own happiness to make sure they felt better.

That version of me grew into a woman who believed that love meant giving more than she received.

Into a partner who thought being patient meant being silent.

Into a mother who thought putting herself last was noble.

Into a daughter who tolerated pain in the name of family.

Into a friend who stayed too long even when her soul whispered, "You deserve better."

Healing forced me to confront all of that.

It wasn't dramatic, no screaming matches, no chaos, no slamming doors. Just honesty. Just moments where I realized: I cannot keep dimming myself for people who do not know how to hold my light.

And one of those people, the most draining of them, left.

Just walked away.

And instead of feeling abandoned, I felt restored.

That was my turning point.

I understood then that waiting for people to change, waiting for them to treat me better, waiting for them to appreciate me, was no longer something I could afford to do. Not emotionally, not spiritually, not as a growing woman learning her own worth.

I am too old to wait for people who are not good for me to choose kindness.

Walking away was never the lesson I learned as a girl, but now it is a skill I choose as a woman.

The Little Girl I Used to Be

Sometimes I picture the younger version of myself, the one who used to sing "The Greatest Love of All" with my sister as we survived childhood together. That song wasn't just a melody; it was a vow we made without knowing it. A vow that we would grow strong even without guidance, that we would teach ourselves how to love when the world failed to show us.

Years later, when I sang that same song at her wedding before I had kids, before I knew the depth of motherly love, something inside me shifted. While she walked into womanhood, I released pieces of a childhood that had weighed us both down. It felt like I was singing her forward and singing our past away at the same time.

That girl who sang with shaky confidence…

She had no idea who she would become.

No idea how much strength she carried.

No idea that she would spend decades trying to make everyone else happy before finally learning how to make herself whole.

But I see her now.

And I forgive her.

Every version.

The Evolution of Loving Myself

Learning to love myself didn't happen in a single moment. It happened in slow, subtle layers:

Through baking the girls' favorite treats on a random Friday and realizing my peace lives in the kitchen.

Through spending hours recording a podcast episode about grace, and finally saying out loud the things I used to swallow down.

Through that first solo trip to New York, sitting at a bar, eating dinner alone, speaking to strangers, realizing I was more independent than I ever gave myself credit for.

I used to think independence had to look like solitude or emotional detachment. But really, it just means trusting myself enough to be alone with my thoughts, to choose my own joy, to sit in my own company and feel safe there.

My creativity, whether it's cooking, recording, podcasting, or drafting this book, has become my home. Not because these things are successful in the traditional sense, but because they allow me to express myself without filtering, without fear, without pretending.

I play with aesthetics, angles, lighting, words, not to impress anyone, but because it feels good to create without the pressure to perform.

It is the most honest version of me.

Marriage, Loneliness, and Reclaiming Myself

Being with someone since your teenage years is both beautiful and complicated. Dave and I have built everything together, a home, a family, a history that spans more than half our lives. But we've also built habits, patterns, and roles that didn't always leave space for who I was becoming. For years, I poured every emotional resource into him, caretaking, supporting, absorbing. It felt natural because that's who I had been trained to be. But it also left me drained, unseen, sometimes lonely inside my own marriage.

Taking my energy back didn't destroy us; it balanced us.

I didn't do it in anger.

I didn't do it to punish him.

I did it because something inside me finally whispered, loudly and firmly, "You matter too."

And what surprised me most was that our relationship did not crumble when I stopped overextending. It steadied. We are traditional; he manages the outside world; I take care of the inside. But now, I do it without losing myself.

We don't have a big circle anymore. Not like we did in Ontario. Life is quieter. Friends came and went. Seasons shifted. And now it's mostly us. Two people who have changed a thousand times but are still choosing each other.

And I believe that somewhere in our future, we will find our spark again, not the spark from when we were teenagers, but a new one that fits the adults we have become.

The Quirks, Fears, and Pieces of Me

There are moments where I forget words and say ridiculous phrases that make the girls howl with laughter, like "wash your teeth" and "brush your face." And I let them tease me because it reminds me that perfection was never the goal. Connection was.

There are moments where the thought of living alone scares me, not because I couldn't do it, but because my entire life has been built around loving others. Silence feels too big sometimes. But I am learning to trust myself with even that possibility, should life ever bring me there.

There are moments when I dream deeply of becoming an influencer of love, healing, and peace. Not for fame. Not for vanity. But for purpose.

I want to be a woman who spreads light.

Who shows others how to heal.

Who teaches through honesty, not perfection.

Who becomes an example of resilience without bitterness.

Who uses her voice instead of dimming it?

And for the first time, I genuinely believe I can.

All these pieces, the mistakes, the clarity, the self-awareness, the dreams, the boundaries, the rediscovery, they are shaping the woman I am becoming.

A woman who isn't afraid of her own power.

A woman who doesn't need approval to exist loudly.

A woman who walks away when energy is harmful.

A woman who forgives past versions instead of shaming them.

A woman who no longer begs for space; she takes it.

A woman who is learning who she truly is outside of motherhood, marriage, and obligation.

Healing hasn't given me perfection.

It has given me truth.

And for the first time in my life, the woman I am becoming finally feels like home.

✦ Reflection & Takeaway ✦

Forgiving yourself is the doorway to becoming yourself.
Every past version of who you were, the girl who tried too
hard, the woman who gave too much, the soul who stayed
too long, was doing the best she could with the love,
guidance, and safety she had at the time. Healing asks you
to honor her, release her, and step into the woman you were
meant to be.

Pause & Consider

Which version of yourself needs compassion rather than
your criticism?

Where have you been dimming your light to fit into spaces
that no longer deserve you?

What changes in your energy happen when someone who
drains you finally leaves your life?

Who are you becoming now that you've stopped apologizing for your boundaries, your truth, and your growth?

Chapter 22: Finding My Voice & Reclaiming My Joy

I've come to realize that my mouth might not always say everything, but my face certainly does. I fidget when I'm thinking, play with my hair, talk to myself, and repeat things as I process them. I am blunt, outspoken, and unapologetically me, and I've learned to embrace it. Singing has become a way to release my emotions, especially while cooking or cleaning. I wear my apron like armor, my music blasting as I move through the rhythm of the kitchen, dancing, singing, and fully present in those moments. The kitchen has become my sanctuary, a place where I can feel fully alive, creative, and connected to myself. In the scent of spices, the sizzle of food, and the hum of music, I find a quiet joy that is mine alone, yet it's also a gift to my family, a way to nourish and nurture through both food and energy.

Playing board games like Monopoly with the girls brings out another side of me, the competitive, playful, and sometimes frustrated side. Just last night, Kierslin bought all my loose ends and refused to trade or sell, leaving me no chance to add houses or hotels. I wanted to quit, but the girls teased me mercilessly for being a sore loser, and in the teasing, I found laughter, connection, and humility. It's these playful moments that reveal the depth of our relationship. We're not perfect, but we're fully present, living in the moment, and finding joy in each other's company. They remind me that life isn't always fair, and yet even in those frustrations, there is love, humor, and the warmth of family.

Sundays have become my sanctuary. I love cooking and cleaning alone, the windows open, music flowing, and the freedom to sing loudly, letting my voice fill the house. The neighbors have complimented my singing, which makes me feel seen in a way that is soft yet powerful. These moments of solitary expression are crucial, a chance to reconnect with myself, to breathe, to dance, and to release everything I've been carrying. They remind me that my individuality isn't lost in motherhood; it's amplified by it. While the girls are occupied, Dave is elsewhere, or I simply choose to be alone, I find peace and clarity. It's a grounding ritual that keeps me centered, even amid chaos or uncertainty.

Travel has been another avenue for reclaiming my independence and assessing my boundaries. I've journeyed through seven states in America alone for work, navigating rental cars, hotel mix-ups, and all the coordination on my own. There were nights sitting in a restaurant, eating by myself, talking to strangers, and realizing that I could rely entirely on my own instincts. These experiences pushed me out of my comfort zone and taught me that independence can be both liberating and empowering. I learned to trust myself in unfamiliar spaces and to take ownership of my decisions without needing validation from anyone else. Those moments of navigating the unknown shaped my confidence and resilience, qualities I carried into motherhood, my creative pursuits, and my healing journey.

Dave critiques my podcast lighting, pointing out its amateur quality, and I laugh it off, telling him I'm just experimenting. It's not about perfection; it's about showing up and playing with the process. Even in these small moments, I practice grace for myself, embracing imperfection as a tool for growth. I allow myself to try, fail, and learn without judgment. My girls watch me, sometimes poking fun at my seriousness or my mistakes, and in those reactions, I see the value of vulnerability. By showing them that I am willing to fail, to laugh at myself, and to continue despite imperfection, I model resilience, self-acceptance, and courage.

Healing has also required me to let go of toxic relationships, particularly family members who tried to shrink me or undermine my energy. Letting go wasn't easy; it took courage to finally release the fear of being unloved or rejected. Walking away from those relationships was an act of self-respect, a declaration that my energy, my peace, and my joy are non-negotiable. The liberation I felt after removing that negativity from my life was transformative. I felt lighter, more alive, and capable of holding space for what truly matters. I realized I am too old to wait for people to leave my life for me; I now take control of what I allow in.

Working with students who confide in me has become another source of healing and purpose. When they share struggles, they face at home, I can respond with empathy, guidance, and understanding. I see reflections of my younger self in their stories, and helping them teaches me the power of resilience, hope, and compassion. Their trust reinforces my sense of purpose and reminds me that I can be a guide, a safe place, and a source of encouragement, a way to rewrite the narrative I once inherited as a child. Teaching, mentoring, and connecting with these students shows me that my own healing isn't just personal; it can ripple outward, helping others navigate life's complexities with strength and care.

Music continues to be a lifeline. Singing has always been more than just a pastime; it is how I release emotions that I cannot put into words. When I cook, clean, or even take a walk, music flows through me. I belt out notes, sometimes perfectly, sometimes horribly, and I laugh at myself. Singing is cathartic, joyful, and healing all at once. Similarly, dancing around the kitchen, losing myself in movement, or even simply tapping along to a rhythm allows me to physically release the tension, the worry, and the fear I've carried. These practices anchor me, remind me of my resilience, and connect me back to the core of who I am.

Even trivial things bring me joy and growth. Late nights playing cards or board games with Dave and the girls, whether it's Monopoly, Cards, or simply taking turns telling stories, feel sacred. Morning coffee with Dave, quiet moments where it's just the two of us, or watching the girls laugh at themselves and each other are treasures. These routines, though simple, are where I find peace, connection, and meaning. It's a reminder that happiness doesn't always come from grandeur; it is woven into small, intentional moments.

Through all this, the music, the cooking, the travel, the games, the podcasting, the laughter, the boundaries, the independence, and the love, I have reclaimed my voice. Not just the literal voice I sing or speak with, but the authentic voice that represents my essence. I've learned to honor myself, to embrace imperfection, to trust my instincts, and to set boundaries that protect my energy. I've come to understand that my joy is not contingent on others' approval, that my healing is ongoing, and that my creativity and self-expression are essential to who I am.

Now, I am more grounded, more expressive, and more attuned to what brings me peace. I embrace the chaos of life, knowing that it is in these moments, laughter, mistakes, music, creativity, and connection, that true growth happens. I continue to nurture my girls, guide them, and share in their lives, but I also honor myself, my passions, and my healing journey. Every song, every meal, every late-night game, and every solitary moment is a testament to the joy and voice I am rediscovering in this season of life.

✦ **Reflection & Takeaway** ✦

Healing blossoms when you honor your expression, protect your energy, and embrace the imperfect yet joyful moments in life. Claiming your voice allows both freedom and connection.

Pause & Consider

How do the moments you carve out for self-expression remind you of your worth and individuality?

In what ways do playful, imperfect, and creative activities deepen your connection with those you love?

How has setting boundaries and releasing toxic influences changed the energy you bring to your life?

Where can you cultivate more sacred rituals, solo or shared, to nourish your spirit and voice?

Chapter 23: When Grief Opens the Door to Deeper Healing

In the previous chapter, I found myself blossoming again, finding joy in my kitchen, in music, in my individuality, in moments with my girls, in reclaiming my independence, and in finally setting boundaries that protected my heart. I was stepping into my voice, fully and unapologetically.

And then life reminded me that healing isn't linear.

It isn't gentle.

It isn't predictable.

Just as I began to feel grounded, I received news that knocked the breath out of me:

Chad was gone.

My cousin, my once-twin flame in humor, chaos, and survival, left this world, and suddenly, everything I had reclaimed felt shaken loose again.

Grief hit me like a wave I couldn't brace for. One minute I was functioning, folding laundry, and humming along to music, and the next I was sitting still, unable to move, feeling a pain in my chest that I didn't know a heart could physically feel. It was like the air changed. Like time softened around the edges. Like my body forgot how to carry this new weight.

I've lost people before, but losing someone who knew every part of my history, the good, the ugly, the hilarious, the broken, felt different.

This loss cut into the foundation of who I was.

Because Chad wasn't just family.

He was the witness to my life.

My favorite person for so many years.

My partner-in-laughter, my fellow survivor, my safe place.

We were both kids raised in chaos, both craving connection, both understanding pain without having to use words. I had siblings, but during the years when my relationship with them fell apart from our mutual brokenness, he was the one I leaned on. He was a single child, and somehow that made our bond even stronger, like we chose each other in a world where so many relationships felt forced or fragile.

And oh, the memories…

They replay in my mind like a movie I wasn't ready to watch yet.

There was that night at my grandmother's birthday, the story we told for years to anyone who would listen. The singer who meant well but… simply could NOT sing. Chad and I locked eyes at the exact moment another family member shouted, "Oh hell no, make it stop!" and we both had just taken sips of our drinks. Drinks sprayed everywhere. The whole table erupted in laughter, and it was the kind of laughing that leaves your stomach clawing for breath. We were ridiculous and absolutely bonded for life at that moment.

That was us.

We lived to laugh.

We could get an entire room going with accents, jokes, and the kind of comedic timing only the deeply broken and deeply aware ever seem to possess.

We were each other's secret-keepers through teen years, relationships, marriages, kids, death, depression, joy. It was the kind of relationship that didn't need maintenance; it simply existed. A soul-tie formed not by obligation but shared experience.

And now he's gone.

The last conversation we had was simple, just catching up, no drama, no heaviness. I didn't know it was the last. That's why it echoes in my mind now. Not because of what was said, but because of what will never be said again.

That's the strange part of grief:

It turns ordinary memories into sacred ones.

It makes you replay small moments, simple words, insignificant expressions, until they become holy.

The pain is sharp.

It's deep.

It radiates through my ribs, as if something is physically missing.

But even inside the pain, something inside me knows this is part of healing too.

Because grief is the other side of love, you don't get one without the other. And when you've loved someone with your whole, messy, complicated heart, losing them hurts in a way that feels unfair. But it's also a reminder that what you shared was real, meaningful, life-shaping.

That's what I want my readers to feel here:

Pain means you lived.

Pain means you loved.

Pain means the relationship mattered.

And grief… grief teaches you to carry people differently.

I've spent years learning to release toxic family members, to walk away from relationships that shrink me, to protect my energy and spirit. But losing Chad wasn't like letting go; it was like someone carving a space inside me and saying:

"This is where he will live now."

And that's what grief is, the creation of a forever-room inside us,

where the people we lost continue to exist

in memory, in stories, in mannerisms,

in the pieces of ourselves shaped by their presence.

He lives in my humor.

In my ability to get a crowd laughing.

In my bluntness.

In resilience, he always admired in me.

In the understanding that brokenness does not erase worth.

In the love I give freely.

In the softness, I show those who need guidance.

And he lives in the ache.

Because ache is love with no place to go.

In a strange way, losing him reminded me of everything Chapter 22 taught me:

How precious it is to have a voice,

How important it is to share your joy while you can,

How healing it is to show up imperfectly,

How necessary it is to love loudly and without apology.

He is gone.

But the love we shared is not.

That part is eternal.

And now, as I continue writing, singing, healing, and growing,

I carry him with me.

In every laugh.

In every memory.

In every moment where my heart reminds me that grief is not a punishment.

It is proof of connection.

Proof of humanity.

Proof of love.

Chad was a gift.

And grief, as painful as it is, has become my way of unwrapping that gift repeatedly, through memory, through storytelling, through honoring the life he lived and the part he played in mine.

I heal by carrying him.

And I love by remembering him.

And the story continues… because love never really ends.

✦ Reflection & Takeaway ✦

Grief is not a sign that something has gone wrong; it is evidence that love existed, that connection mattered, and that your heart was brave enough to let someone in. When someone you shared history with leaves this world, the pain you feel reflects the depth of your bond. Grief can be healing when you allow memory to become a source of light, not just loss.

Pause & Consider

Where in your heart do you still carry the people you've lost?

How can you honor their memory through the way you live, love, and express yourself today?

What has grief taught you about love, connection, and the meaning of presence?

How might you allow both the ache and the gratitude to exist together without diminishing each other?

163

Chapter 24: When Grief Teaches You How to Live Again

There is a strange quiet that settles into your life after someone you truly love leaves this world.

It isn't silence; silence can feel peaceful.

This is different.

It's a shift in the air, a soft rearranging of who you are, like the universe gently but firmly insisting that nothing will ever be quite the same again.

After losing Chad, I kept thinking about Chapter 23 and all the ways I wrote about carrying him forward. But what I didn't expect was how his loss would change the way I carried everything, my relationships, my dreams, my fears, my boundaries, my anger, my tenderness. Chapter 23 cracked open something deep inside me. Chapter 24 is where I started to understand what was coming through that crack.

Grief isn't breaking my heart; it's reshaping it.

It's forcing me to slow down, to soften, to reflect on what I have been moving through before the world shifted under my feet. All the joy I've been reclaiming, the voice I have rediscovered, the boundaries I have set, the independence I have been nurturing, those things suddenly feel both more fragile and more sacred. Losing someone who knew your childhood laughter, your secrets, your stages of becoming forces you to confront the truth that healing does not pause for grief, and grief does not pause for healing. They walk together, hand in hand, shifting their weight back and forth like a dance you never agreed to learn.

Before Chad passed, I had been blossoming again, singing more, laughing more, letting my creativity be messy and imperfect and mine. I was rediscovering the version of myself who had been buried under decades of responsibility, survival, and emotional suppression. But after the news settled deep into my bones, it felt like the universe was asking:

"Now that you remember what matters, what will you do with the life you still have?"

I didn't have an answer at first.

All I had were memories.

His laugh.

His way of telling a story.

The way he could pull the humor out of absolutely anything.

How easy it was to be myself around him.

How our childhood wounds stitched us together in ways even our families didn't fully understand.

And yet, as I moved through the days after his passing, I noticed something happening in the background of all the pain:

I was living more intentionally.

I was listening more carefully to my own voice.

I was paying attention to the softness in my daughters' eyes.

I was noticing the way Dave reached for me, even in small, quiet ways.

I was allowing myself to cry without apologizing for it.

And I was letting myself laugh even when the guilt tried to tell me I shouldn't.

Grief has a strange way of sharpening your vision.

You suddenly see people differently.

Choices differently.

Time is different.

Your own heart is different.

It made me think of everything I had said in Chapter 22, the rediscovering of my voice, the joy I'd been reclaiming, the vibrancy returning to my life. That chapter was about rising.

Chapter 23 was about breaking.

Chapter 24 is about becoming.

Because grief, when you allow it to flow through you, forces you to stop living on autopilot. It makes you look at what you're holding onto and what you need to release. It made me reevaluate how I love, how I speak, how I show up, how I rest, how I dream. It made me notice where my energy was being drained and where it was being nourished.

And suddenly, all the things I had been learning, setting boundaries, valuing joy, reclaiming creativity, forgiving myself, speaking honestly, felt less like lessons and more like survival tools.

Grief taught me what joy really meant.

It taught me what love really meant.

It taught me what presence meant.

It taught me that legacy is not just what people leave behind; it's what they ignite inside you.

Chad left me with a truth I didn't fully understand until now:

We are here to love each other into becoming who we're meant to be.

Not to fix each other.

Not to save each other.

Not to shrink ourselves for each other.

But to expand, to grow into the fullest versions of ourselves through the people who walk beside us.

And now, as I walk forward, I feel him in the quiet moments.

When I laugh too loudly.

When I tell a dramatic story.

When I sing in full voice with the kitchen windows open.

When I choose joy without asking permission.

When I speak up instead of staying small.

When I show my girls it's okay to break and rebuild.

He is still here, not in his body, not in his voice, but in every part of me that remembers love as something wild, honest, and deeply human.

Chapter 24 is where my healing meets my grief and realizes they are not opposites.

They are partners.

And together, they are teaching me how to live again.

✦ Reflection & Takeaway ✦

Grief not only breaks us open, but it also expands us. It becomes a teacher, reshaping how we understand time, love, purpose, and legacy. Through loss, we begin to see what matters with a clarity we never asked for but desperately need.

Pause & Consider

How has grief sharpened your understanding of what truly matters in your life?

What parts of you began to grow only after something or someone was lost?

How do you carry the love, lessons, and laughter of those no longer here?

What does living fully look like for you now, in this new season of becoming?

Chapter 25: The Return to Myself

There is a point in healing when the noise quiets, the doubts, the outside opinions, the ghosts of old habits, and all that's left is the truth about who you are.

I didn't realize I had reached that point until I looked around my life and saw something I never had growing up: a family that chooses each other, willingly, consistently, joyfully.

Our home has shifted into a place where connection feels natural, not forced. We are planning holidays together, something that used to feel like a burden but now feels like a celebration. Not because everything is perfect, but because we've built a rhythm where our togetherness is intentional. We're not surviving each other's schedules. We're prioritizing each other's presence.

Last night was proof of that. It was supposed to be simple: pick a movie. But in typical family fashion, it took thirty minutes of "not that one," "I've already seen this," and "scroll back, that looked good!" We debated, laughed, got irritated, and then laughed again. Eventually, I held up the remote and said, "Okay, democracy isn't working, we're watching this one." They all groaned, but they settled in instantly. Leadership sometimes looks like knowing when to stop the chaos before it spirals.

I curled into Dave's side as the movie started. His arm found me without searching. He reached for my hip the way he does when he's relaxed, lightly, affectionately, like a reminder that he sees me even in silence. He traced gentle patterns with his fingers, grounding me in peace I didn't know how to accept years ago. I fell asleep like that, the girls stretched out across the recliner and the other couch, the room dim and warm with the sound of a family simply being.

Growing up, neither Dave nor I had this.

Not at our girls' ages.

Not even close.

My own relationship with my mother was complicated; love was there, but timing wasn't always. I moved out at fifteen, carrying a mix of independence, hurt, and stubborn resilience. Years later, when we lived together again, it wasn't the seamless reconnection I imagined. She was busy rebuilding her own life, and I was doing the same. We loved each other, but we didn't always meet in the middle. And for a long time, it left a mark on me, a quiet ache for the mother-daughter closeness I would later fight to create with my girls.

That's the thing about generational healing:

It demands intention.

It requires choosing differently, even when the blueprint doesn't exist.

It asks you to build what you never received.

And slowly, beautifully, we are doing that.

The girls come to me more freely now for advice, for comfort, for laughter, or simply to be near me. Dave and I have softened into a mature love where presence speaks louder than performance. We talk more. We listen more. Our home feels like a space where emotions aren't judged but welcomed. Where conflict leads to understanding, not fear. Where love is not conditional or fragile.

The truth is, we didn't get here by accident.

We got here because I stopped letting voices infiltrate our marriage, our home, our peace.

There was a time when noise, people's opinions, projections, whispers, and disruptions threatened the foundation Dave and I worked so hard to build. The kind of noise designed to divide. I didn't realize how much space it assumed in my mind until I finally shut it out and heard my own voice again. The clarity that followed was liberating.

Almost shocking. It allowed me to see my marriage for what it truly was: not broken but buried under distractions not meant for us.

Removing that noise forced us to rise into a new maturity, the kind that isn't loud or dramatic but steady and chosen. The kind that makes love feel like a partnership instead of a performance. The kind that deepens intimacy in the smallest moments, like a hand resting on my hip during a movie I barely stayed awake for.

And somewhere in the middle of all this healing, I found something I thought I had lost:

my artistry.

Creativity used to be effortless for me, a natural part of my identity. Singing, storytelling, performing, expressing… it lit me up. But life buried those parts of me under layers of responsibility, trauma, and survival. For years, I lived on autopilot, doing what needed to be done while ignoring what made my soul feel alive.

Now, that part of me is waking back up.

I feel it when I sing in the kitchen with the windows open.

When I record my podcast, even imperfectly.

When I write.

When I allow myself to dream again.

When I choose curiosity over fear.

There is a fire returning to my creativity, slow but undeniable.

A reclaiming.

A remembering.

A rebirth.

And with it comes determination.

Real determination.

Not the frantic kind, fueled by fear of failure,

But the grounded kind, rooted in purpose.

I am committed to following through with my ideas, my healing, my growth, my creative work, and the life I'm building with Dave and the girls. I'm no longer trying to prove myself. I'm simply returning to myself.

This chapter feels like the moment in a long journey when you stop looking back and finally look forward, clear-eyed, steady, sure. I am no longer shaped by what broke me. I am shaped by what I'm choosing to create.

A healed home.

A connected family.

A maturing marriage.

A creative woman rising again.

This time, with intention.

This time, with confidence.

This time, fully awake to the truth of who I am.

And I can finally say:

I'm home.

In my family.

In my marriage.

In my art.

In myself.

✦ **Reflection & Takeaway** ✦

Healing deepens when connection becomes intentional, and when you choose to build a life rooted in presence instead of the patterns you inherited. Rediscovering your creativity and strengthening your family bonds are not separate journeys; they are reflections of the same truth: you are returning to yourself.

Pause & Consider

Where have you mistaken noise for truth in your life, and what shifts when you finally quiet it?

How does intentionally choosing connection with your partner, children, or inner self reshape the way you experience love and safety?

In what ways are you breaking generational patterns and building something your younger self never had?

How is creativity trying to re-enter your life, and what would happen if you made space for it without judgment or urgency?

What small moments, a movie night, a hand on your hip, shared laughter, remind you that you are already living a life your past self prayed for?

Where can you honor your emergence by following through on the goals and dreams you once put aside?

Chapter 26: Rebuilding, Resilience, & Creative Roots

Our family has grown into a rhythm that feels intentional, grounded, and full of love. Weekends are when we truly try to anchor ourselves together through meals, conversations, and laughter. Despite the challenges of our schedules, commuting for work, and the girls' extracurriculars, we make it a priority to sit at the table as a family. It's not always perfect. Sometimes it takes thirty minutes to decide on a movie to watch, like last night, until I finally made the choice for us. But those moments are ours. I fell asleep nestled into Dave's side while he tickled my hip, the quiet intimacy grounding me in a way I didn't know I could experience.

Looking back, I realize that none of this existed in the same way with our parents at our girls' ages. Dave and I didn't have that closeness with our own families. Even my relationship with my mother had its ebbs and flows, years when we couldn't connect, followed by periods of reconnection as she grew on her own path. Now, I am consciously mending generational patterns. I am creating a family ecosystem where connection, presence, and love are the currency, not just the rhythm of life happening around us.

I am emerging into the creative soul I had tucked away for so long. Cooking and my podcast aren't just hobbies; they are expressions of my essence. I experiment with flavors, recipes, and techniques, each one a manifestation of my love for my family and for myself. I sing in the kitchen, apron on, loud music, dancing, and laughing at my own ridiculous moves. The girls tease me for my seriousness, but I know they are absorbing the lesson I've learned: it's okay to be fully yourself, even when the world tries to tell you otherwise.

Dave and I have also found a new balance. We've reached a point where we anticipate each other's needs without many words. Snowy mornings are easier because he brushes the snow off my car when time permits; I make his lunch every day. We give and receive small acts of love that reinforce our connection. Spending time apart allows us to miss each other and rediscover the spark, making our time together even more intentional. We've learned to coexist in a way that doesn't require constant explanation; we simply understand and show up for each other.

The girls are blossoming, and their growth fuels my own. Friday nights spent with Merhye working on her social media design, mornings and evenings helping Kierslin study or simply guiding them through homework and life lessons, all of it reminds me of the role I play as both guide and witness to their independence. I am proud of how they absorb the love I give, not just from me but from the example I set by pursuing my own passions and creative pursuits.

Healing has been an integral part of this chapter of life. I've learned to step back from gossip, negativity, and distractions. I no longer entertain mean-spirited behavior, and I actively protect my energy. It's taken years to realize that allowing people to drain me does nothing but limit my joy, creativity, and family connection. Walking away from toxicity without guilt, without doubt, has been one of the quietest victories of my life.

Creativity has become the heartbeat of my day-to-day life. Podcasts are a place where I speak my truth, share my vulnerabilities, and release what weighs on my heart. Cooking has become more than just a meal; it's a ritual of love, patience, and expression. The aroma of fresh bread, the sizzle of soups, the comfort of early winter soul foods: all of it connects me to the life I am intentionally building. Each act of creation is both a gift to my family and a reclaiming of myself.

As a family, we are more connected than ever. Holidays are planned together, board games and card nights are sacred, and the laughter that fills our home is a reminder of why all the struggles, planning, and juggling are worth it. Our unspoken bond grows stronger with every shared moment: meals, laughter, missteps, and small victories alike. We've built something that our younger selves could not have imagined: a home where love, respect, and joy are the constant threads.

The internal transformations are subtle but undeniable. I am more resilient, consistent, and confident. I no longer chase perfection in myself or expect it in others. I recognize my values, my voice, and my energy, and I protect them fiercely. I guide my girls not by sheltering them from life's complexities, but by showing them how to navigate it with grace, humor, and authenticity. And in the process, I've reclaimed parts of myself I thought were lost forever: my creativity, my voice, my ability to prioritize joy, and my capacity to love fully while maintaining my boundaries.

This chapter of life is about building intentionally, healing collectively and individually, and embracing the messy, imperfect, joyful journey of family, creativity, and self-discovery. The path isn't always smooth, but it is ours, and that is everything.

✦ **Reflection & Takeaway** ✦

Family, creativity, and personal growth are intertwined in ways that are both grounding and transformative. Healing, setting boundaries, and prioritizing joy create a foundation from which love can flourish.

Pause & Consider

How does intentional presence with your family deepen connection and shared meaning?

In what ways are your creative pursuits an expression of your identity and a tool for healing?

Where can you set boundaries to protect your energy while still nurturing those you love?

How have resilience and consistency shaped your confidence and internal strength?

Which rituals, shared or solo, bring you the most clarity, peace, and joy, and how can you expand them?

Chapter 27: The Quiet Becoming

There is a quieter kind of becoming that doesn't announce itself. It doesn't demand witnesses or validation. It arrives in subtle shifts in how I move through my days, in how I speak to myself, in how I no longer feel the urge to explain or defend who I am becoming. This season feels less like survival and more like alignment. Less like striving and more like grounding.

I've learned that growth doesn't always feel like progress. Sometimes it feels like repetition. Like choosing the same values repeatedly, even when it would be easier to abandon them. I no longer expect immediate success or instant clarity. I've made peace with the slow build. Consistency has become my quiet rebellion against the version of myself who used to give up when things didn't bloom right away. Now, I stay. I tend. I trust.

That shift has changed everything.

Our home carries that energy now. We try, intentionally, to eat together, especially on weekends, knowing how much our schedules work against us. Long commutes, extracurriculars, and responsibilities pull us in different directions. Still, we try. We sit. We share food. Sometimes it's chaotic, sometimes rushed, but often it's grounding. Those meals are my love language made tangible. The food I cook isn't about trends or presentation; it's about care. It's about creating a space where everyone can exhale.

My food content has grown from that same place. It's not performative. It's not curated perfection. It's real food for real people, my family. Comfort meals. Soups, bread, and dishes that warm more than the body. Cooking feels like me again. Like artistry rooted in nurture. It's where my creativity meets my instinct to care, and that combination feels sacred.

My podcast holds a different kind of expression, but it comes from the same source. It's about healing, open, honest, unfiltered. I speak about what rises in my chest, what life is teaching me in real time. I don't wait until I've healed something completely to talk about it. I talk from within the process. That honesty has become my purpose. I'm no longer trying to sound polished; I'm trying to sound true. Healing doesn't require perfection; it requires presence.

Dave and I have reached a depth I didn't know was possible. It didn't come from eliminating challenges; it came from choosing each other through them. Watching our girls reach milestones, witnessing who they're becoming, and celebrating their individuality, that has bonded us in a way nothing else could. We became more intertwined through shared pride, shared worry, shared hope.

Somewhere along the way, Dave allowed me to lead our parenting journey. He saw my ambition, my forward-thinking nature, my instinct to build something better than what we were given. That trust didn't create an imbalance; it created harmony. We now move as partners who understand each other's strengths without needing constant explanation. There's an unspoken rhythm between us; one built on respect and shared intention.

Internally, I feel steadier than I ever have. I've reached an age where I understand that resilience matters more than brilliance, and consistency matters more than intensity. I tell my girls this often: all you need to do is try and stop trying to be perfect. Those words are as much for me as they are for them. I live them now. I allow myself to be human. To learn as I go. To grow without self-punishment.

Motherhood has become leadership for me, not control, not perfection, but guidance. Modeling what it looks like to show up imperfectly, to stay committed, to protect your energy, to build a life rooted in values rather than noise.

Dave and I are consciously creating what we never had, a connected family culture where love is shown, not assumed.

This chapter of my life feels creative, connected, and purposeful. I see a future where financial freedom comes not from burnout, but from alignment, doing work I love, work that heals, work that feeds both my family and my soul. I'm not rushing toward it. I'm building it, brick by brick, day by day.

The quiet becoming isn't flashy. But it is powerful. It is rooted. It is honest. And for the first time in my life, I trust that who I am becoming doesn't need to be rushed; it needs to be honored.

✦ **Reflection & Takeaway** ✦

Becoming isn't always loud. Sometimes it's choosing consistency over urgency, honesty over performance, and alignment over approval. Growth rooted in love, creativity, and resilience creates a legacy that lives far beyond achievement.

Pause & Consider

Where are you being invited to slow down and trust the process instead of rushing outcomes?

How can your everyday rituals, meals, conversations, and creative expression become acts of legacy-building?

In what ways are you leading, not by control, but by example?

What might financial freedom and purpose look like if they were built from alignment instead of pressure?

Chapter 28: Becoming the Change, We Leave Behind

I used to think legacy was something reserved for later, something measured after life had settled, after stories were complete. Now I understand that legacy is not a finish line. It is a living, breathing thing. It is built in ordinary days, in quiet decisions, in the way you choose to heal and the way you choose to love.

If I am remembered for anything, I hope it is this: how I healed, and how I loved.

I hope my girls say I had a big heart. That I was a good mother, one who sacrificed, supported, and stood beside them while they chased their dreams. That I made space for who they were becoming instead of trying to shape them into something safer or smaller. I want them to know that I always put them first, not by losing myself, but by becoming strong enough to lead them forward with intention and care.

There are patterns in families that feel almost inherited, as though they live in the walls, in the blood, in the silence between generations. I made a conscious decision to break them. I broke the cycle of teen pregnancy. I broke the pattern of abuse by never laying a hand on my children. I broke the habit of pretending everything was fine when it wasn't. I broke the silence that teaches children to hide their pain. I broke the pattern of guilt, never making my girls feel responsible for my emotions or my happiness. And I broke the cycle of victimhood, choosing accountability over blame, healing over resentment.

One of the hardest patterns to break lived inside me. For years, I believed I was worthless. That belief was planted early, spoken aloud when I was too young to protect myself from it. It shaped my confidence, my voice, and the way I measured my value. Healing meant challenging that lie repeatedly. Now, when doubt creeps in, I speak back to myself with compassion. I remind myself that growth requires failure, and failure requires bravery. Trying is no longer something I fear; it is something I honor.

What feels most new in this season is grace. I show it more freely now to others and to myself. I listen instead of reacting. I pause instead of defending. I try to understand instead of assuming. This grace has softened me without weakening me. It has made my relationships more honest and my inner world more peaceful.

My marriage has grown alongside me. The shift wasn't dramatic; it was subtle, steady, and earned. Dave began showing up in ways that mattered to me, and I learned to meet him with patience instead of expectation. Emotional safety became our foundation: Not using anger as a weapon, not being cruel when we are hurt, and allowing space for expression without judgment. It feels like falling in love again, but this time with awareness. This time with choice. This time with two people who finally see and know each other.

Cooking found me when I needed grounding. At first, it was simply nourishment, feeding my family, creating comfort. Then I started sharing it, and people responded. They encouraged me. They asked for more. I realized cooking is my love language. When I am in the kitchen, I am joy, presence, and care all at once. It is where I feel the most alive and connected.

The podcast became another lifeline. When I threw away the script and spoke from my heart, something shifted. My voice stopped feeling performative and started feeling real. Talking about healing, about life as it unfolds, gives me a place to release what I was carrying. I am not afraid of where either of these paths might lead. What excites me is their potential, the way they can grow if I continue to show up, stay consistent, and trust myself.

Motherhood has taught me that leadership doesn't come from control; it comes from example. I tell my girls that perfection is not the goal. Effort is. Consistency is. Being true to yourself is. I want them to compare themselves to who they were yesterday and no one else. I want them to see failure as growth and relationships as something to cherish and protect. Much of what they learn from me is unspoken; it lives in how I try again, how I recover, how I keep going.

Protecting my energy has become essential. I no longer allow gossip, hatred, or judgment to assume space in my life. I trust how people and situations make me feel. Alignment matters. Peace matters. I choose to nurture what lifts me and walk away from what drains me without guilt or apology.

When I imagine my life five years from now, success looks different from what it once did. It is work I love, creative, meaningful, and fulfilling, paired with financial freedom that allows generosity instead of fear. My home feels calm and restorative. My inner life feels steady and full of love. Abundance means having more than enough and sharing it freely.

I am no longer waiting for the world to change. I am becoming the change I want to see through healing, through love, and through the life I am intentionally building for myself and my family.

✦ **Reflection & Takeaway** ✦

Legacy is created through daily choices, how we heal old wounds, how we love those closest to us, and how bravely we break the patterns that no longer serve us. Change begins within, then ripples outward.

Pause & Consider

What patterns are you ready to end so something healthier can begin?

How can you speak to yourself with more compassion when you fail or fall short?

In what ways can grace become a daily practice rather than a rare one?

How are you already becoming the change you hope future generations will inherit?

Your healing matters. Your love matters. And the life you are building, one intentional choice at a time, is already leaving a legacy.

Chapter 29: What They Will Carry Forward

Lately, I find myself thinking less about what I am building and more about what will remain. Not the tangible things, homes, schedules, accomplishments, but the quieter imprints. The way love sounded in our house. The way conflict was managed. The way mistakes were owned. The way safety was created, not demanded. Legacy, I've learned, isn't something you leave behind. It's something you live out loud while people are watching.

My girls are watching. They are watching how I speak to myself when things don't work out. They are watching how I manage disappointment, how I recover from exhaustion, and how I apologize when I am wrong. They are watching how I love their father, how I hold boundaries, how I choose peace over chaos, even when chaos would be easier.

There was a time in my life when I believed being strong meant being silent. When surviving meant swallowing discomfort and moving on without question. I carried that belief into early motherhood, into marriage, into relationships that asked me to shrink to belong. But healing has rewritten that narrative.

Strength now looks like honesty.

Safety looks like openness.

Love looks like accountability.

I no longer pretend our family is without struggle. I no longer shield my girls from hard conversations or uncomfortable truths. Instead, I invite them into them, age-appropriate, respectful, grounded in trust. I want them to know that life is not about avoiding pain, but about learning how to move through it without losing yourself.

One of the most important patterns I've broken is silence.

My girls know they can talk to me about anything: fear, anger, confusion, desire, mistakes. There is no topic that requires shame in this house. There is no emotion that must be hidden to be loved. That openness didn't come naturally to me; it came from unlearning the belief that my voice didn't matter.

I spent years believing I was worthless because someone said it with authority. It took time, years, to realize that words spoken in cruelty are not truth; they are wounds.

Healing didn't erase the memory of those words, but it stripped them of their power.

Now, when I fail, I talk myself into trying again.

When I fall short, I remind myself that growth lives there too.

When doubt creeps in, I answer it with effort.

I want my girls to see that progress matters more than perfection. That consistency is not about never faltering, but about returning to yourself repeatedly.

There is also a gentler version of me emerging, one that offers grace more freely, not because people deserve it, but because I deserve peace. I no longer meet anger with defensiveness. I no longer internalize behavior that has nothing to do with me. I've learned that understanding doesn't require self-abandonment.

My marriage has changed because I have changed. The shift wasn't loud. It didn't arrive at a dramatic moment. It happened quietly. When Dave began showing up in ways I needed, and I softened enough to receive it. It happened when I chose patience over keeping score, and when emotional safety became more important than being right.

We are relearning from each other, not as teenagers, not as exhausted young parents, but as adults who have lived, lost, grown, and stayed. Emotional safety now means we can speak without fear of cruelty. It means anger doesn't become a weapon. It means we are allowed to be human without punishment.

I feel like he sees me now.

And more importantly, I see myself.

The legacy I hope to leave is not about success or recognition. It's about love practiced daily. Healing modeled openly. Effort honored. Grace extended.

I hope my girls say I have a big heart.

That I supported their dreams without trying to live through them.

That I sacrificed without resentment.

That I loved them loudly and protected them fiercely.

I hope they remember a mother who tried.

Who owned her mistakes.

Who broke cycles instead of repeating them.

Because how I healed and how I loved will matter long after the details fade.

And that, I believe, is enough.

202

✦ Reflection & Takeaway ✦

Legacy is not built in milestones, but in moments. It is shaped by how we respond, how we repair, and how we love when no one is asking us to perform.

Pause & Consider

What patterns are you consciously breaking for the next generation?

How do your daily responses teach others what love and safety look like?

In what ways can honesty and grace coexist in your relationships?

If those you love were to remember one thing about you, what would you hope it is?

Chapter 30: The Life I Am Choosing

There is quiet confidence that comes when you stop asking for permission to live the life that feels true to you. I didn't arrive here all at once. This version of me was shaped slowly through motherhood, marriage, grief, mistakes, forgiveness, and the daily decision to keep showing up even when I wasn't sure where I was headed.

For most of my life, I believed I had to earn peace. That happiness came after success. That rest was something you were allowed once everything else was overseen. Healing taught me otherwise. Peace is not a reward; it's practice. And happiness is not found at the end of the road but woven into how you walk it.

The life I am choosing now is intentional.

I choose presence over pressure.

I choose meaning over momentum.

I choose depth over noise.

I no longer chase every version of who I could be. I am learning to stand firmly in who I am becoming. A woman who loves deeply, creates freely, sets boundaries without guilt, and allows life to unfold without forcing it into shape.

Motherhood remains at the center of my world, but it no longer consumes my identity. My girls are growing into themselves, and I am growing alongside them, not behind them. I no longer measure my worth by how needed I am. I measure it by how grounded I remain as they step forward.

Watching them balance their lives, school, work, friendships, and passions, fills me with a pride that is both fierce and peaceful. They are good humans. Thoughtful. Kind. Capable. And I know that whatever lies ahead for them, they will walk into it with integrity.

My marriage, too, feels different now, not perfect, but rooted. There is a steadiness between Dave and me that didn't exist before. We have learned how to miss each other, how to return to each other, how to choose connection without force. Love no longer feels like something I must hold together alone.

And then there is me.

The woman who cooks because it feels like love.

The woman who speaks because silence costs her too much.

The woman who creates not to prove, but to express.

I am choosing a life where my work reflects my values. Where financial freedom is a tool for peace, generosity, and security, not status. Where success feels expansive, not exhausting.

I am choosing to trust that what is meant for me will meet me where I am, not where I pretend to be.

This chapter of my life is not about arrival. It's about alignment. And for the first time, that feels like enough.

✦ **Reflection & Takeaway** ✦

There comes a moment when healing shifts from something we work on to something we live. Not because everything is resolved, but because we finally trust ourselves to carry what remains. Choosing your life doesn't mean having it all figured out; it means standing rooted in who you are, even as the path continues to unfold.

Pause & Consider

What does alignment look like in your life right now, not perfection, but honesty?

Where are you still asking for permission to choose yourself?

What parts of your life feel grounded, even if they are still growing?

If you stopped striving and started trusting, what might become possible?

What version of yourself are you ready to commit to not someday, but now?

208

Author's Note

If this book found you… This book was never meant to be perfect. It was meant to be honest.

I wrote these pages while still healing, still learning, still unlearning. I wrote them as a mother, a wife, a woman reclaiming her voice, and a human who has known both deep love and deep pain. If you found pieces of yourself in these chapters, then this book did what it was meant to do.

Healing is not linear. Growth is not clean. Love is not quiet.

If there is one truth I hope you carry with you, it is this:

You are allowed to change.

You are allowed to take up space.

You are allowed to walk away from what hurts.

We do not heal by becoming unrecognizable; we heal by becoming honest.

If you are still figuring it out, you are not behind.

If you are tired, you are not weak.

If you are choosing yourself, you are not selfish.

May this book remind you that your story matters, your voice matters, and your healing, however messy, is worthy.

Thank you for sitting with me through these pages.

9 781970 577938